Henny and Lloyd
Fight Crime

John Paulits

Henny and Lloyd Fight Crime

"Before Jessica turned eighteen, she ran away. Just up and left, along with some of her Stuyvesant friends. Warren spent a boatload of money trying to find her. He found out approximately where she was, somewhere in Maine, but he never managed to pinpoint her, much less bring her home. Let me assure you, he never stopped trying to find her, never stopped loving her, never stopped hoping for that one magical phone call or knock on the door. But it didn't happen. Then we got word that she was dead. An unexplained accident in the Maine woods. By the time the Maine authorities in Cotters Grove, the nearest town, had investigated and learned her antecedents and sent the news to Warren, she'd already been buried. He never saw her again after she left home at seventeen. Didn't even get a chance for a final farewell."

"How long ago did you say her death occurred?" I asked.

"Jessica would have been twenty when we received word of her passing. And that would be some eighteen years ago, the summer of 2006. Warren had nothing after that but his work. For those previous three years, though, he'd searched for her, hoped for her, constantly. He wasn't a religious man, but I know he prayed for her to return. But..." Towers shrugged and looked down for a moment. "You mentioned his will. He never changed his will. Well, that's not strictly true. Whatever slim ration of hope he lived on, hoping for Jessica's return, was the belief that the report of her death was in error. Since he'd never seen her since she originally left, the door for a miracle remained open, if only a crack. In his will she was his sole, number one beneficiary. If, however, she truly was dead, he left a list of others who would share in the inheritance. I should tell you he was cremated, according to his wishes."

Towers stopped talking. I felt a vague premonition about what was coming next, and asked, "And what is the problem now with the inheritance?"

"Jessica has come back to claim it."

"The dead daughter?" Henny sputtered.

"Yes and no," Towers answered. "She says she is Jessica Goldman. But I don't believe her."

Henny and Lloyd
Fight Crime

John Paulits

A Wings ePress, Inc.
Detective, Crime Mystery

Wings ePress, Inc.

Edited by: Jeanne Smith
Copy Edited by: Bev Haynes
Executive Editor: Jeanne Smith
Cover Artist: Trisha FitzGerald-Jung

All rights reserved

Names, characters and incidents depicted in this book are products of the author's imagination or are used fictitiously. Any resemblance to actual events, locales, organizations, or persons, living or dead, is entirely coincidental and beyond the intent of the author or the publisher.

No part of this book may be reproduced or transmitted in any form or by any means, electronic or mechanical, including photocopying, recording, or by any information storage and retrieval system, without permission in writing from the publisher.

Wings ePress Books
www.wingsepress.com

Copyright © 2024 by:
ISBN 979-8-89197-984-0

Published In the United States Of America

Wings ePress, Inc.
3000 N. Rock Road
Newton, KS 67114

Dedication

To Becky Lee and Act Two

One

There was nothing to do but stare out of the window. The day before, Monday, starting in the afternoon and lasting into this morning, snow swirled through the air and Mother Nature's cold shoulder provided a modicum of visual entertainment, but not an entire workday's worth. I heard very little automobile traffic pass by our Centre Street building, which the Henny and Lloyd Detective Agency call home and where Henny and I sat, wondering what to do with ourselves. No sirens screamed 'get out of the way;' no car horns shouted coded obscenities at one another. Our office phone had rung once in two days, and, not owning an automobile, I told the caller we had no desire to extend our manufacturer's warranty. New York City had grown quiet, and I didn't much like it.

But all bad things come to an end, and Henny and I cast one another a look when we heard the building's clanking, decrepit elevator clang and bang itself into action. I'd phoned Henny earlier that morning before we left our Brooklyn apartments, and, after talking it over, we decided that, since the subways were running, why not go to the office, despite the slim possibilities the day offered for a new client falling into our hands, or considering the conditions outside, slipping and sliding into our office. We'd get through the day somehow. I had my hand-me-down-from-Henny book to read, *The Corpse with the Blistered Hand,* from 1940 by a fellow named R. A. J. Walling, whom I googled and found had written a slew of mystery novels in the thirties and forties. Henny had a knack for finding these eighty- and ninety-year-old tomes and always made them available to me. Most of them were not bad. Very few were terrific. Anyway, Henny had his toothpicks to play with, one always stuck in the corner of his mouth, and we both had the snow swirls to look at. And, despite the snow, Henny still wore one of his double-breasted pinstriped suits, complete with fedora.

We'd learned to recognize the moans and groans of our elevator and knew it had stopped on the third floor, our floor.

"What do you think?" Henny asked in a soft voice.

"A lost soul trapped on the streets looking for a restroom?" I answered.

Then someone knocked, and Henny, his desk nearer the door, rose and welcomed the gentleman inside.

"I'm dripping all over your floor," the man apologized. "So sorry." He spread his hands to indicate his helplessness to correct the situation.

Henny took yesterday's *NY Post* from his desktop and spread it out on the floor near our guest.

"Toss your things on the newspaper," he said.

The man complied, and I watched the newspaper suck up most of the moisture and hoped Henny would volunteer to clean up the mess the man would leave behind. Our client chair sat in front of Henny's desk today—we traded off, one day in front of his desk, the next day, mine—and the man sat with a notable sense of relief. He seemed about forty years old, maybe a little more, and dressed in a blue sweater over a white, collared shirt and jeans. He wore leather boots, the bottom half of which were darkened by the wet snow he'd slogged through.

"Can I get you some coffee?" I offered.

"Oh, yes. That would be wonderful," the man answered, his voice a little higher than it should be.

Henny settled behind his desk and asked, "What can we do for you? It must be something pretty important to bring you out in this weather. Let's start with your name."

I put the cup of coffee where our guest could reach it, along with two little containers of half and half and two envelopes of sugar.

As he spoke, he fixed his coffee. "My name is Randall... Spoon?"

"Randall Spoon?" Henny repeated.

"What? No," our guest said. "My *name* is not Spoon. I *need* a spoon."

I got up and went for the spoon I should have remembered in the first place.

"Thanks. My name is Randall Givens."

I listened to the *clink clank* of the spoon against the sides of the cup and wondered when Randall would get down to business.

"You're right about it being important to bring me out on a day like this... I'm pretty sure it is, but..." he shrugged, "...it's been bothering me." He sipped from his cup. Henny gave a sigh I felt like echoing, but I restrained myself. I was eager to hear, but Randall seemed loath to explain.

"Tell us what brought you here," I urged.

"Yes, of course." He set his coffee cup down on the edge of Henny's desk. "I picked up a hitchhiker yesterday morning. Before it began to snow." He gestured toward our windows where the snow show appeared to be abating. "I stopped at the service area around milepost ninety on the Jersey Turnpike. The sky was dark and obviously some weather event loomed."

Weather event? I repeated to myself. Hoity toity.

"I wanted to fill up my gas tank before it did and decided to get some coffee and a snack. Inside, sitting at one of the tables I noticed a young man, probably in his early twenties, studying each person who entered the building. He had a duffel bag at his feet, but he was nicely dressed. Not a bum or anything like it. He reminded me of when I was in college and trying to travel somewhere, although he looked too old to be in college. I'm talking some twenty years ago as regards myself. Depending on the kindness of strangers, if you will, for a ride.

"I'd been driving for a while already yesterday morning—coming up from Baltimore—and, well, he and I got to talking and I asked him if he needed a ride. I mentioned to him about my college memory. Anyway, he said he'd had some bad luck lately, and he'd be most grateful for a ride—and a meal. He added the comment about the meal with some embarrassment, so I bought him a chicken sandwich and French fries. Long story short, he was trying to get to New York City. I told him it was my destination, too, so we teamed up, and I drove him into the city and dropped him on one of those little streets in Chinatown. Henry Street it was. You're not far from there yourselves."

"We know where it is," Henny said. "We often get lunch from over that way."

"Yes, well. It was a little out of *my* way—I live in the Village, West Eleventh Street—but it had already begun to snow, and I couldn't see making the young man walk from the Village back downtown carrying his bag through the weather. You know what I mean?"

I'd hoped something interesting might come of Randall's visit, but it didn't appear to be in the cards. "And you're telling us this, Mr. Givens, because...?" I asked.

"When I finally got home—you see I park in a lot—I checked in the back seat where the young man—he said his name was Jimmy—had thrown his duffel and found this." Randall pulled a long, white envelope from his back pocket. "Read it," he said, passing it across the desk to Henny.

I watched Henny take a folded sheet of paper from the envelope and read silently. A tiny furrow appeared atop his nose, and I knew Henny well enough to know his attention had been captured. He lowered the paper, looked at Randall, said, "I presume this isn't yours, and you believe Jimmy left it in your car."

"It's definitely not mine," Randall assured us in his mild-as-buttered-toast tone. "And no one's been in the back of my car for I don't know how long. It had to have come from my passenger."

Henny rose and stepped my way. I took the paper from him and read the printed-out communication.

You thought I was kidding, didn't you? I said I'd come back and find you, and now I have. I write this letter in case you're out or don't open your door. It won't matter. I don't care. You've abandoned me for the final time. You've robbed me for the final time. You've crushed my very heart for the final time. You've humiliated me for the final time. Now I will crush you. If you've run, I'll chase you down. If you're simply ignoring me, it won't be for long. If I've slipped this under your door, then the next time you leave your apartment will be the last time. And I'm so looking forward to making it happen.

I glanced at Henny. "The envelope?"

He held it up. Blank. He said, "It wasn't even sealed. Just had the flap tucked in."

Henny said, "What did your passenger—Jimmy?—do when you dropped him off?"

"I saw him go up the stoop to the front door of the building he wanted, but then I drove away. A truck was coming up behind me. Slippery street, you know. I didn't want the truck sliding into me. That's the last I saw of him."

"Why are you coming to us?" I asked. I waved the letter a little. "This does sound threatening. You should take it to the police."

Randall shook his head and rose. He stepped to my desk and retrieved his letter. "I don't like dealing with the police. And no way they'd take this to heart. I'd get shunted from officer A to officer B to officer C, and then to the front door and the sidewalk. You know how they are."

I explained. "You understand, we charge for our services. The police don't."

Randall gave a grunt. "And you get what you pay for. I can give you a few hundred dollars."

"To do what?" Henny asked. "You dropped Jimmy off in front of a building on Henry Street in a snowstorm." He flipped a hand over and gave Randall a "what now?" face. Randall frowned. He still stood in front of my desk, the letter in his hand. He folded it and slid it into his pants pocket, leaving the envelope lying on Henny's desk. "I'm only trying to be a good citizen. If you're not interested, you're not interested. My conscience is clear."

"Don't be offended," I said, rising. "Here, take this." I handed him one of our cards. "If anything else comes along, or if you hear any more from this Jimmy, let us know. From what you've told us..." I shrugged.

Randall took the card I offered and slipped it into his pants pocket. "Sorry to have troubled you." He retrieved his wet coat from the newspapers on the floor and let himself out.

"He came out into a snowstorm to tell us that?" Henny asked. "Good citizen or crazy loon?"

I plopped back into my desk chair and ignored the question. "It provided a break in the day, at least."

We heard our elevator go into action.

Henny sighed. "Where are the long-lost days when a sultry blonde enters the office with a delicious little problem on her hands?"

"Gone. Along with most of your other 1940s' fantasies." Henny is a great aficionado of the classic mystery era. Classic to him. When he dressed up, which was pretty much always, he wore double-breasted, often pinstriped, suits and never went anywhere without a fedora on his head. As I mentioned, his taste in literature was limited to mystery novels of the thirties and forties. I gave Henny a smile. "Don't worry. One day a vamping siren will walk through that door and change your life."

"Fat chance." He popped a toothpick between his lips and spread out an array of them on his desk. I opened *Blistered Hand* and asked, "Are we coming into the office tomorrow?"

"Not if it's still snowing," Henny said.

I agreed and returned to reading.

The snow, however, stopped later in the afternoon, and after a brief cell conversation the next morning, we decided to head to the office. Good thing we did, because around one in the afternoon, a petite knock sounded. Henny shuffled the toothpicks from his desktop into the desk drawer and went to open the door. When he did, she walked in.

Two

"Do you mind if I smoke?" were the first words out of her mouth. From the way Henny was eyeing her, I don't think he would have minded if she'd set his wastebasket on fire. She wore no hat, and her wavy blond hair cascaded over her ears to her shoulders. Wrapped in a fluffy, white coat that reached to her knees, she might have passed for the abominable snowman's wife—and a lucky abominable snowman he would have been to have a wife so un-abominable. She turned her back to Henny and opened her coat. He obeyed and slipped the coat from her shoulders and went to hang it on our coat rack next to his fedora.

"Please," I said, gesturing to our plush client chair, today placed before my desk. The young lady—she couldn't have been more than twenty or twenty-one—was dressed in a sweater and tight ski pants, the day having turned out sunny and brisk, and wore boots that ended an inch or two below her knees. And she was pretty.

A howl from Henny shocked both the young woman and me. He'd failed to close his top desk drawer completely, and when he did so now, he caught his pinky in it. He threw us a lopsided smile and rubbed his finger. Then, even though the young lady had already taken our client chair, he said, "Please, sit." Following another lopsided smile, he looked my way for help.

Something you need to understand about Henny besides his predilection for classic *noir* mysteries and the glamour that accompanies them. He had a strange longing—strange to me, anyway—to have a reciprocal explosion of immediate passion with a sultry new client. He'd dated a couple of previous possibilities whom we'd helped with their problems. He'd wanted to date other possibilities who brought their problems to us, but never had the chance. Boyfriends, husbands, and their general lack of interest spoiled his fantasy. What made it worse—worse for Henny but better for me—was the fact that I'd met Susan Denzler on one of our very early cases. Susan worked for a Chinatown newspaper which translated her articles for publication. The case on which we'd met and which she wrote about launched her onto the *New York Post*, where she'd written quite a few stories of note, a couple of them involving Henny's and my encounters with evildoers. Also, she'd been of great help to us in ferreting out solutions to other cases of ours, something that irked me a bit since Henny and I were the detectives, not her. At any rate, she and I had grown close since then—very close, but Henny now was looking to me for some help.

"What brings you to us today?" I asked.

"What's your name?" Henny blurted. I tossed him a quick frown when the young lady looked his way.

"My name is Daria. Daria Givens. And yours? Ashtray?"

She wasn't suggesting that Henny's name was Ashtray. She was requesting one. Neither Henny, addicted as he was to toothpicks, nor I smoked, so I quickly put a paper cup on the edge of Henny's desk where she could reach it. Noting the look she tossed me, I made a mental note to splurge on an ashtray for the office.

"You may call me Henny."

Daria extracted a cigarette from a shiny, silver case and waited, the cigarette dangling from her fingers. She offered both of us a frown and lit her own cigarette with a shiny, gold-colored lighter. I imagined Henny vowing to splurge on a lighter for the office.

"And I'm Lloyd," I added. "How can we help you?"

Daria blew out a long stream of smoke, then nestled the cigarette between her lips and searched inside the small purse she had in her lap. She extracted a business card and pushed it toward me. It was one of ours. I lifted it to show Henny, then returned the card to her and said, "You said your name was Givens?"

"I did. Daria Givens."

"We had a gentleman visit us yesterday..."

Henny interrupted with, "In the middle of the snowstorm."

Daria glanced at him. "It snowed yesterday. I know that." Henny nodded and returned to silence. "Yes," she went on. "He's my uncle. May I ask what he wanted of you?"

This was a touchy question. Although we hadn't accepted Randall Givens' business and so weren't particularly bound by any code of silence or loyalty, it still seemed a breach of ethics to me to share his story with anyone. Henny, though, was not so morally inclined.

"He was worried about a hitchhiker he picked up on the Jersey Turnpike the day before."

"Concerned? How so?" Another elegant stream of smoke wafted from Daria's full lips. She crossed her legs.

I tried to give Henny a cautionary look, but his eyes were locked on Daria, and he went on.

"He found a threatening letter in the back seat of his car which he thought could only have been left by his passenger. He found the letter after he dropped the young man off in Chinatown."

"I see. What did he want you to do about it?"

Daria gave a toss of her hair, and it was enough to mesmerize my partner, so I said, "Your uncle felt he needed to inform someone... because of the nature of the letter."

"The nature of the letter?"

"It had a threatening tone," I repeated.

"I see. So, this stranger left behind a threatening letter, and my uncle brought it to you? Who did it threaten? Him? And what did he want you to do about it?" she repeated.

I gave a slight shrug. "No, not him. No one specific. It sounded like a lovers' quarrel. As to what to do about it, we never actually got that far. We directed him to the police, but I got the impression he believed he'd done his duty by informing Henny and me and had no interest in going to the police."

Henny came back online. "We did what Lloyd said. Told him to take it to the police. We've done nothing regarding it."

"There wasn't anything *to* do," I added. "The only name your uncle had for the passenger was Jimmy. He dropped the man in front of an apartment building and then drove away. There really was nothing for us to do." She rose and dropped her cigarette butt into the paper cup.

"My coat," she said softly, smiling at Henny.

Henny popped up and retrieved her fluffy white coat. He spread it open and after Daria backed into it, he managed, "Isn't there anything we can do for *you*? Don't you want to leave your contact information."

Daria faced him while she buttoned up. She gifted Henny with another small smile and said, "No, I don't think that will be necessary. I'll be in touch."

She stepped toward the door, and Henny nearly bowled her over getting ahead of her so he could open it.

"Bye," she said, her eyes on Henny. "For now." She grasped the outer doorknob and gently pulled the door closed, leaving my partner staring at our frosted window.

"Want to sit back down?" I asked.

Henny turned my way. "Wow!"

"You liked her, did you?"

"Wow!" He staggered to his desk chair. "It's like someone opened my brain, searched my dreams, and *poof!* There she stood."

I laughed. "Now, there she *doesn't* stand."

"She said she'd get in touch again."

"Not exactly."

"She did." He quoted her, complete with her breathy intonations. "'Goodbye. For now.' You heard her."

"I did. You're right."

"She'll be back. I know she will. And she's not married."

I frowned. "And you know that how? I noticed no rings, too, but not everyone wears their wedding ring nowadays."

"She's got the same name as her uncle. Family name. Birth name. She doesn't have a husband, or she'd be Daria Somebody-Else."

"Randall could be her uncle-in-law, and she's a Givens by marrying into the family."

Henny glared my way. "She said 'uncle,' not 'uncle-in-law.'"

I shut up and allowed Henny his fantasy. It was a slow day and popping dream bubbles didn't seem to me to be a sociably appropriate thing to do, under the circumstances. As it turned out, though, Henny was right. We soon heard from her again.

~ * ~

Randall Givens visited us on a Tuesday, Daria on Wednesday. On Friday we received an email to our office address from Daria inviting us to a get-together (her term) on Saturday evening at her loft on Nassau Street, downtown not far from our office. Henny opened the email and after reporting the contents to me said, "I told you so. She says I should bring my assistant." He gazed at me, lifted his eyebrows, and smiled. "And we each may also bring a plus one." His smile melted. Naturally, I would invite Susan. Try as he might, Henny's only plus one was the face he saw in the mirror each morning.

"She doesn't mean I'm to be your plus one, does she?" I asked.

"No, no, no. We may each bring a plus one."

"It's better for you if you don't have a plus one. If you did, it would eliminate your making Daria your future plus one."

Henny nodded sagely. "Yeah. When she sees me show up solo, she'll know what it means." I doubted she would but, you know, dream bubbles again. "Oh, I didn't scroll. There's another sentence. She says she may have some business for us."

"Good, we need it," I said. If Henny's and my bank accounts were gas tanks, the *low fuel* light would be shining. Winter was hard on us all. "Does she say what the business might be?"

"Nope."

"Does it mention the occasion for the get-together?"

"Nope."

"Does it give a time?"

"Eight o'clock."

"I'll give Susan a call. We can have an early dinner at Giandos." Giandos was our go-to fancy restaurant, walking distance from Henny's and my apartments.

I spoke to Susan and arranged the night.

"I'm looking forward to this," Henny said. "It could turn into something big."

It did.

Three

Early Saturday night, Susan met Henny and me at the bar in Giandos for dinner. The bar always seemed less restrictive and more casual and convivial than the spread of tables across the floor of the restaurant. Then we made use of Susan's *NY Post*-sponsored Uber account and found our way to Nassau Street. The building Daria had directed us to appeared to have been put to some industrial use in a previous incarnation. We took the elevator to the fourth of the six floors and found Apartment C. I knocked and a gentleman unknown to me opened the door, drink in hand, and welcomed us with a strange effervescence.

"Come in, come in," he bubbled. "The more the merrier. I'll tell Daria you're here." He took two steps then turned back. "Who shall I say has arrived?"

"Henny and Lloyd," I informed him.

"Henny and... Lloyd. I see." He stepped away, and I felt I had knocked some of the effervescence out of him.

We were in a very large room whose ceilings must have been twelve feet high. Small knots of people were spaced around the floor. A long table with sandwiches, chips, pretzels, cheese, dips, stood in the middle of the room. Another table loaded with various bottles of alcohol and mixers stood deeper into the room, a white-jacketed bartender dispensing the drinks.

"Swanky," Susan whispered.

"Not a bad way to live," Henny replied. I looked for Daria, and after a moment or two I saw her coming toward us, a broad smile on her face, her hair pulled into a ponytail secured by a bright red ribbon.

She took Henny's hand and said, "I'm so glad you could make it on such short notice."

"Thanks for asking us," I answered, when Henny appeared to be descending into cardiac arrest. Daria dropped his hand, and he became respiratory again.

"Yes," Henny managed. "It's nice to be here."

"This is my friend, Susan Denzler," I said, introducing the two ladies. "She's a reporter for the *New York Post*. Susan, this is Daria Givens." While the girls greeted one another and got acquainted, I quickly studied the guests. A young crowd surrounded us. For a moment I thought Henny and I, only twenty-seven, might be the seniors in the group, but there were a couple of clearly older men talking together near the drinks table. But only a couple.

Henny had calmed enough to engage in conversation with Daria, so I redirected my attention his way as he asked her, "Will your uncle be here tonight?"

"Uncle Randall?" Daria replied. "I invited him. I always do. He and I are actually alone in the world. The last of the Givens... or the Givenses. I wish to be correct before a professional writer." She and Susan exchanged smiles. They were genuine smiles. I detected no cattiness.

"Come get a drink," Daria offered. We followed her to the drinks table, where we made demands of the bartender, and she refreshed her own drink before guiding us off to the side where a sofa and three upholstered chairs allowed us to sit. The noise level was low, and we continued our conversation. Or at least I did.

"How did you know your uncle came to see us the other day?"

Daria crossed her legs, sending her tight red skirt higher by a few inches as her right foot, clad in a spiky, red high-heeled shoe, dangled enticingly a few inches off the floor. I assumed this pose would keep Henny mute for a few moments, but Daria had begun to explain. "I mentioned that Uncle Randall and I are, what you might call, alone in the world. I feel responsible for him. He needs... well, to be honest, he needs to be monitored."

"Monitored?" I repeated. "What do you mean?" Susan, I noticed, was listening closely.

Henny appeared to be listening, but I knew his mind was otherwise engaged and I'd probably have to fill him in later.

"He's functionally... light-headed." Daria giggled. "Thank goodness he doesn't need to work for a living. He can take care of himself and all of that. But he sometimes sinks a little below the waterline... or rises a little above the clouds. When he returned from Baltimore, for example..." She paused and smiled at Henny. "Can I get you something? A sandwich? Don't you like your drink? I can get you something else."

"Drink? No, I have a drink." Henny held up his glass.

"You don't seem to have taken even a sip yet." Daria's smile was constant.

Henny quickly sipped some of his gin and tonic. "I... I was listening to your story."

Daria gave a quick laugh. "You can listen and drink at the same time."

"I do. I mean I will."

"Anyway, I stopped over Uncle Randall's apartment when the snow let up to check on him. Your card was lying on his coffee table, and he was feeding his turtles. I asked him about the card, and he mentioned he went to visit you with a problem. Naturally, with Uncle Randall involved, I wanted to find out what was going on, so I pocketed your card."

"Didn't you ask him?" I posed.

"He was too involved with his turtles."

Susan interjected. "Your uncle keeps turtles?"

Daria gave an eye roll. "Don't ask. His place is full of them. I think he drove to Baltimore for something to do with turtles. Probably to pick up another one. It's a passion of his."

"I'd like to see them," Henny said. "I had a turtle when I was a kid. The little kind with the red ears."

"He has a few of those," Daria said.

I asked, "You said he doesn't have to work. Are you responsible for him financially?"

"No. He and I both share the family inheritance. Givens Pharmaceuticals. We sold the concern to a Canadian company when my parents, Uncle Randall's brother and sister-in-law, were killed in a plane crash."

"When was this?" Susan asked.

"Four years ago. Both he and I are very well set for a lifetime. I like to celebrate that reality once a month." She gestured with her arm to indicate that such a monthly celebration was now underway. She got to her feet. "I need to mingle. Feel free to eat and drink." She giggled. "And carouse." The final two words she directed at Henny, who lifted his glass in a toast.

As she walked away, Henny leaned toward Susan and me. "Do you think she's taken with me? A little?"

I gave Henny a nod. "She did seem to have a marked preference for you and your comfort. She noticed you hadn't touched your drink."

"I know. I know," Henny said, a thoughtful glaze coming over him.

With a smile, Susan added, "Take your best shot, Henny. Ask her out. If a twosome is too much pressure, make it a foursome. You'll volunteer, Lloyd, won't you?"

"I will if you'll be the fourth."

"She said she might have business for us," Henny said. "That's an easy opening to go and talk to her again."

Being the more business conscious of us two, I said, "Do that. It appears she can afford a decent fee. I wonder what she could want, though."

"I'll bet it has something to do with Uncle Randall," Susan said.

"You may be right," I agreed. "He is a bit of a mystery. Oh, and there he is."

Looking over the food array stood Randall Givens, dressed in a powder blue shirt and gray pants, white China plate in his hand.

"No turtle soup on the menu, I'm sure," Henny said.

"Why the devil are we here?" I burst out.

"Gentlemen," Susan cautioned. Then she laughed. "There is a table offering sweets. Enjoy your drinks; have another. I'm getting dessert." She walked off.

"This is all very nice," I said, "but we don't really know anyone. Daria has to go about hostessing." I shrugged. "Look, go remind Daria she said she might have some work for us. The office rent is due, and I'd rather pay it with new money than money we already have." Henny was somewhat lax in his approach to finances. He had a generous, or more properly put, a large, sympathetic streak in him that I'd often had to curtail for the sake of our fee. "Look, why don't you go talk to your girlfriend and ask if she was serious about offering us a job."

"You come with me."

"You won't make much progress in romance dragging me along."

"We'll talk about business, and if you sense the topic changing to something more enticing, you can go look for Susan."

I agreed. Leaving Henny on his own might end up with him volunteering to solve Daria's problem, if she had one, as a gesture of good faith and a romantic lure, but the young lady seemed to have money to burn or to at least to feed her friends once a month, and to my eyes she didn't need charity of any sort. We headed off toward Daria, who stood in the center of half a dozen young men and women, laughing up a storm.

When she noticed Henny and me circling, she excused herself and joined us.

"I hope you're enjoying yourself," she greeted. "I see your friend Susan has found the dessert table. Please, help yourself."

"We will," I assured her. "You're a busy lady tonight seeing to your guests. You did mention you had some work we might do for you."

"We'll be glad to do what we can," Henny added.

Daria sighed. "My uncle's arrived." She bobbed her head toward Randall, who stood talking to the two older men I'd noticed earlier.

"Who are his friends?" Henny asked.

I would let Henny take as much charge as he was able.

"I don't know," Daria replied.

"Didn't you invite them?" Henny asked.

"No. I always tell Uncle Randall to invite a few of his friends if he'd like. He doesn't have very many. He must have invited those two. I suppose I should go and greet them. Later. I'm always hopeful he'll invite a woman he's met, but that never happens. I'd like to see him get married and settle down. She'd likely clean the turtles out of his life."

"Him, a wife, and turtle makes three," Henny added.

"Three!" Daria exclaimed, her eyebrows bouncing upward. "And turtle makes a hundred and three."

I spoke. "Seriously? He can't have so many turtles, can he?" I tipped my head back and squinted at Daria. "Your exaggerating, right?"

"Well, maybe a little. Maybe not a hundred, but if you ever have reason to visit him, you'll really get an eyeful. And often a nose full."

"Sounds like a quiet hobby, at any rate," Henny said softly.

Daria gave a laugh. "That's one positive about it, I guess. But yes. What I wanted to suggest... There's nothing I want done exactly right now, but as I said, I have to keep an eye on Uncle Randall. He's capable of going off on tangents... doing odd things. Once, he bought a truck and had it fitted out to transport his turtles—he can't go away without finding someone to babysit and feed his turtles and give them 'the love they need.' My uncle's words."

"He doesn't ask you?" Henny put to her.

"He knows better. I have other things to do than clean up turtle poop." She laughed again.

"What about the truck?" I asked.

"He spent a mint decking out the inside for the comfort and ease of the turtles, but it didn't work out. Water splashed, turtles got bounced out of their... cages or fishbowls. Whatever you call the things they live in. He had to give it up and couldn't find any normal human being who'd take a turtle-mobile off his hands, so he donated it to the Bronx Zoo. Money down the drain."

Daria paused and neither Henny nor I could think of anything to say.

She continued. "If I catch him in anything like the truck fiasco, I'd want you to try to stop him. If *you* catch him considering any such ridiculous thing, I want to know about it. I'd want you to keep an eye on him. Not that you need to follow him around night and day, but check on him once in a while, you know. See where he's going and what he's doing. Is that possible? Can you do that?"

I spoke before Henny could offer his generous heart to her and agree to help her out as a favor. "I'm sure we could, but this doesn't sound like a one-time assignment. It seems you want us to be ongoing sentinels over your uncle. I don't know how much time we can devote to him. We often have other items we need to attend to that are more immediate."

"Can I put you on some kind of... retainer? You give Uncle Randall whatever time you can. I don't expect you to do this for free." Daria screwed her lovely mouth up into a thoughtful pose for about five seconds. "Would a thousand dollars a month be fair? Naturally, I'd like occasional reports—say every two weeks—about what he's up to. If he goes off the rails, I'll be there to try to reason with him and talk him out of any foolishness. You understand?"

"We do," I assured her, thinking contentedly of Daria paying two-thirds of our office rent every month into the near future. I clapped Henny lightly on the shoulder. "I'm going to join Susan for dessert. Daria, you and Henny can talk over the specifics of things. I'll catch up with you later," I promised Henny, nodded to Daria, and went to find Susan.

I paused when I saw her talking to the two men Randall Givens had supposedly invited to the gathering. Randall himself wasn't in sight. When I checked, Henny still had Daria's attention. The two men with Susan shook hands with her and headed for the door.

"Who were they?" I asked Susan after I'd grabbed a chocolate chip cookie.

"You won't believe who. I think I might do a story on them and Uncle Randall."

Susan wiped some chocolate from the corner of my mouth with a napkin she still clutched. "I was saving that for later," I said. "Go on.... the two men?"

"Randall, it seems, is thinking of donating a ton of money to build a turtle preserve along the waterfront in Baltimore. Those two gentlemen are lawyers he's using to do what needs to be done. The Bronx Zoo turned him down."

I explained to Susan about Daria's wanting Henny and me to keep an eye on Randall.

Susan said, "I wonder if she knows he's hoping to endow a Givens Turtle Center in Baltimore."

"Just your saying that makes this whole experience sound ridiculous. Why don't you try to interview Randall? Daria said his apartment is full of turtles."

Susan laughed. "Just *your* saying *that* makes this whole experience sound ridiculous."

I could only join in with her laughter.

"Shall we tell her about her uncle's plan?" Susan said, a twinkle in her eye.

Before we'd taken even a step toward Daria, we saw her lead Henny to a desk in a corner of the room.

"It looks like a checkbook she's taking out of the drawer," I said.

"Now she's grabbed a pen," Susan added.

"Maybe we don't want to interrupt her at the moment." I put my hand on Susan's back and directed her to the drink table. "Your next gin and tonic is on me."

"Cosmopolitan, if you will."

"As you wish. Nothing is too good for you."

Drinks in hand, we moved to a quiet spot. Daria and Henny had separated, and Henny scanned the wide room and found us.

"This should be interesting," Susan said and sipped her Cosmo.

Henny lifted a finger to us and went to get a drink. When he joined us, he said, "She gave me a check. A thousand bucks to keep an eye on her uncle. And a thousand for many months ahead."

"Maybe not," I said and explained the Baltimore connection.

Henny's cheerfulness slid away. "Oh. She's going to want us to prevent him from doing that, you think?"

"Very much I think," I agreed. "She'll at least want to be informed of it, if she isn't already, which I don't think she is."

"Where is he?" Henny asked. "Did he leave?"

"He and his two lawyers are gone."

Henny looked at Susan.

"What?" she asked.

"Any ideas?"

Susan smiled. Apparently, she enjoyed drinking Cosmos. But I already knew this. She said, "I'm going to do an article, or at least make like I'm writing one, about Randall and his animal generosity. Don't do anything until I interview the two Givens family members and the lawyers. One of them gave me his card. Let me set an appointment with Daria before we leave. It'll save me from chasing her down on the phone tomorrow. I'll deal with the uncle later."

Susan clicked my glass and walked away.

"I'm taking Daria to dinner tomorrow night," Henny said. From his tone, I expected him to burst out in song.

Just to be annoying I asked, "She said yes?"

He answered with a scathing look. "Why wouldn't she?"

"No reason. Good for you," I complimented. "You need Susan's and my backup?"

"No, no. I don't think so."

"Giandos?"

"Of course, and don't you show up. I can handle this. I think she's really into me."

It was my turn to click Henny's glass. "Go for the gold, pal." We wandered through the party making small talk where we could. I kept my eye on Susan and figured out she'd succeeded when I saw her and Daria shake hands. It left me wondering, though, what Henny and I were going to have to do to earn our monthly thousand dollars.

Four

Henny tossed his gray fedora toward the coat stand. It bounced off the wall without coming in contact with a single, upturned metal prong. "Just once," he muttered. "You'd think, just once."

I'd left Henny to himself on Sunday, figuring if he changed his mind about going solo with Daria, he'd call, and I'd track down Susan, who told me she'd be very busy this weekend, and we'd help him navigate his Sunday dinner with Daria. But Henny stayed quiet over the weekend, and while he looked forward to Sunday evening, I looked forward to Monday morning and a full report.

I preceded him to the office by about fifteen minutes.

"Don't your hats get dirty spending so much time on the floor?" I asked. "Want coffee?"

"No and yes."

"Uh, no to the floor and yes to the coffee?"

"Correct. You'd make a good detective, Lloyd."

As I waited for the coffee machine to fulfill Henny's order, he asked, "When did you say Susan is interviewing Daria?" He already had a toothpick jutting from the corner of his mouth.

"Daria is giving Susan lunch in her apartment today at twelve, and at three, she's going over to visit the uncle."

"Turtle city?"

"Yep. In his apartment. I'll be eager to hear what *that* was like. Here." I placed Henny's coffee down in front of him. "And in between she's stopping in to see Detective Thursday."

"Why him?"

"Looking for a story," I explained. "We and she have helped him. He's reciprocating by letting her drop by once in a while for news—if there is any." Detective Thursday was an NYPD detective for whom we'd help break a case or two. Allowing him to take credit—Susan played up his part in the handful of stories she wrote about the crimes—had bound him to us. Henny especially liked the sense of having an insider on the police force who appreciated a two-way sharing of information. Very *noir,* he told me more than once.

"But you're avoiding the elephant in the room," I said. "How did last night go?"

Henny smiled at me. "Fantastic. Daria's really sweet. She's as sweet as she is pretty. God, her long hair..."

"She's plenty pretty," I confirmed.

"And she's plenty sweet," Henny added.

"What'd you two talk about?" Henny and I could spend hours at a time in the office and not say a word to one another, not out of attitude or pique, but simply because we had nothing particular to say. I hoped he did better with Daria.

"We talked all night. About everything! Once we started, we couldn't shut up. It was great."

"Did the topic of her uncle and the turtle conservatory arise? Or anything about what she expected for her retainer?"

"Her uncle, some; her retainer, not a word; the turtle

conservatory, not a word. She didn't bring it up, and if she didn't already know about it, I didn't want to be the one to spring it on her and have the evening end up in the toilet. She'll no doubt hear about it from Susan today."

"From your bubbly spirit, I presume there will be a second date?"

"Already arranged. Unfortunately, she insists that you and Susan come along."

"Gee, thanks. When I tell Susan, I'll leave out your 'unfortunately.' Is there a time picked out for this dinner?"

Henny beamed another smile my way. "Daria said she'd be happy to see me anytime. She wants you and Susan to pick the evening. She'll have dinner for us in her apartment."

"She'll cook?"

Henny waggled his head back and forth in mock arrogance. "She'll have someone in to cook it."

"She said?"

"She said," Henny confirmed.

"Nice," I said softly.

"I know it's only one date, but I really like Daria."

"Yes, you said. I don't blame you."

Henny and I sank into our usual quiet mode, both of us probably thinking about his date, and the day went by without a knock or a phone call to distract us. Around four-thirty, though, Susan called to make certain Henny and I were still in the office and said not to leave because she'd be with us shortly and had some news.

For a few moments, Henny and I tried to guess the news, but gave up and sank back into quietude until the rattle of our vintage elevator sent me to our office door. I stepped into the corridor and watched Susan exit the elevator and walk my way. I closed the door behind us and returned to my desk. Susan went to the coffeemaker and plugged in a pod.

"What's the big news?" I asked.

"I think I have a client for you. Give me a minute." Coffee in hand, Susan moved our client chair closer to my desk and set her cup down. "First, you're probably going to have to start earning your retainer. Daria didn't know the two gentlemen Uncle Randall invited to her party were involved in trying to establish his turtle habitat in Baltimore. She kept under control, but the smile on her face dropped to the floor with a loud thud. She didn't want to talk about it. The interview declined from there, and I could sense her blood pressure rising the longer we sat together. As soon as lunch was over, I took my leave. She attempted to send me off with a smile as I exited, but, uh-uh. Worst smile ever."

Henny said, "That's the case you've brought us. Prepare for Daria?"

"No, no, no. I have more."

"You went to see the uncle, didn't you?" I asked.

"Wow! His whole apartment is turtles. You wouldn't believe it. It's a first-floor apartment in a brownstone and has the use of the backyard, which is also for his turtles. Bowls, aquariums, everywhere. *He* wasn't the least bit reluctant to discuss his 'Baltimore project,' as he called it. The cost will be in the low millions!"

"That'll thrill Daria," Henny mumbled.

Susan went on. "And he had a young lady with him. Attractive enough, but you've met him. He's over thirty and kind of a nebbish, but his money talks."

"What did the young—I presume she was young—lady look like?"

"Very sweet woman, maybe twenty-five. He introduced her as Lucy Lyons. Her chief responsibilities seemed to be smiling and gushing over Randall's green, four-legged apartment mates. I would guess Randall treats her well. She had on a bracelet—the kind without a clasp you simply slide your wrist into. Shiny silver with one great, green stone in the center. Wouldn't mind having one of those myself." Susan looked my way. "Hint, hint. Anyway, when she praised his 'Baltimore Project,' by parroting his own words, I knew she, shall we say, was in his thrall. He owned her."

I asked, "When you interviewed Daria, did she bring up her uncle's lady friend? Does she know about her? At the party, she mentioned hoping Uncle Randall would marry, settle down, and get his mind off of turtles. Maybe the girlfriend will take the sting out of the turtle habitat news."

"No, no mention. She did say he'd had a run of girlfriends, but nothing lasting." Susan gave a quick laugh. "She added that she much preferred him spending their money on women rather than on turtles."

"You'd think Uncle Randall would prefer that too," I said.

"At any rate, afterward I visited Detective Thursday. This news will be more in your line. He had an angry, *very* angry man on his hands. The man, his name is Paul Beckman, was with Thursday when I arrived, and I heard them standing outside Thursday's office. Later, Thursday told me Beckman's daughter had been murdered in her apartment somewhere downtown. Before Beckman left, I heard him call Thursday and the NYC police incompetent and say he intended to hire some private investigators who could find out who murdered his daughter. Thursday told me he gave Beckman your card, so don't be surprised if he shows up here."

"What did Thursday tell you about the murder?" I asked.

"Young woman named Nancy Beckman, a would-be writer who worked in an insurance office doing paperwork and such. She'd had two pieces published in a children's magazine. Her father went on about how hopeful those two successes made her before her world came crashing down."

"How was she murdered?" Henny asked.

"Blow to the head. The body wasn't found until people in her office alerted her father she hadn't shown up for work and hadn't called in. He went to the apartment and used his key. You can imagine."

"I don't think I want to," I said. The room stayed quiet for a moment. Finally, I brought Susan up to date on our invitation to Daria's for dinner.

To Henny, Susan said, "Better check and see whether she's still comfortable with having me. Today was awkward."

Henny nodded, and I sensed him slipping into a funk.

Susan rose. "Well, gentlemen, that's all I have for you. We'll keep in touch." She walked around my desk to kiss me goodbye, then let herself out.

"Why is life so complicated?" Henny muttered in my direction. His cell chimed. "Daria."

I listened to Henny's end of the conversation. He didn't have much to say, but when the call ended, he looked my way. "She'll be here within the hour. Turtle Village has upset her."

Henny spent the next five minutes in front of the small mirror we'd hung on one wall of the office and then the next twenty straightening up his desktop and the office in general.

"Want me to run out for some Danish?" I asked when he sat down at his desk.

"What do you think she'll say?" he asked, my sarcastic Danish suggestion dying at birth.

"Well, she may want to know why Susan knew about the millions-of-dollars turtle home, and we didn't. And if we did, why didn't we tell her, since that's what she's been paying us for the past couple days. Our retainer may slip down the drain over those issues." Before Henny could respond, I raised a cautionary finger to him and said, "Or... she'll want us to put a stop to Uncle Randall's plan, and I don't see how in the world we'll ever be able to do that. Again, there goes our retainer."

"Geez, our glass doesn't make it to half full. We don't even have a glass." Henny slumped in his chair. "How about we say we sent Susan to tell her the news. You know—girl-to-girl."

"We'll have to tell her something. Let's see how it goes. I'll help you out all I can."

Henny glanced at me and offered a thankful nod.

Five

"Oh, Henny," Daria cried after taking one step into our office. Henny closed the door gently behind her. "I'm so glad you're here." She grasped Henny's upper arms and pulled him close for a discreet hug.

"Of course I'm here for you," Henny whispered. I heard the whisper, of course, but they separated, and Henny led her to our client chair, which I'd moved in front of his desk upon the news of Daria's imminent arrival.

"What's this all about?" Henny asked. Both he and I were anticipating a blowup by Daria over our not letting her know about Uncle Randall's turtle plans. Fortunately, the blowup never came.

"Have you heard?" Daria glanced my way. "Your friend Susan must have mentioned my uncle's crazy plan for his damn turtles."

I answered. "She did call me a little while ago. Henny and I have been discussing what to do about it."

Henny draped her hooded parka on our coat rack, then reclaimed his chair. The emotional buzz of Daria's arrival had subsided some, so I took a moment to look her over. Her upset had not, it seemed, extended to her dressing haphazardly and rushing over to us. She wore a short skirt and silky blouse. Her low-rise boots covered her to just above her ankles. She'd applied makeup. Then I recalled she'd come from the interview with Susan, and I made a mental note, later forgotten, to ask whether Daria had dressed like this for her.

"Can't you do anything to help me?" Daria asked, piercing Henny with her gaze.

I gave Henny a moment, but when his answer was slow in coming, I said, "We need to know more about this. Susan tells us it's a million-dollar endeavor."

"More than a million! God knows how much. He won't do it on the cheap. I've told Uncle Randall he can't go around spending money like... like someone's minting it for us. We live on the earnings of the money my father left us. If the capital goes down—and it has because of him, and it will plummet with this turtle nonsense—then our income goes down. He has no sense. I maintain a certain lifestyle, and I don't want it watered down or destroyed by my nutty uncle. I've thought of having him put away somewhere, but he spent another boatload of our money on lawyers and shut me down quickly on that."

I asked, "Can't the two of you split whatever money you have, and you can let him dig his own grave?" I didn't like hearing the "grave" part come out of my mouth. "So to speak," I added, to soften the effect.

"My father wrote his will specifically to keep me as a babysitter for his baby brother. We share. My father made sure to take care of him when he was alive, but he left it to me to take care of him after he passed by binding us together with the inheritance. But Uncle Randall is out of control. He won't listen to me. He won't be sensible." She tapped the side of her head. "He's soft where it matters."

Daria gathered herself and continued. "I've talked myself blue in the face to him, but he puts on his usual vapid smile and tells me not to worry. If he goes overboard with this turtle thing, I don't know what we're going to do. Maybe he can sell his apartment and live in a terrarium alongside his turtles."

Daria had worked herself up again. When Henny looked my way, I put my thumb to my mouth and tipped my hand up.

"Daria," he said, "would you like something to drink? Coffee, water, a drink?"

"No, no, thank you. Maybe tonight I'll take refuge in some booze."

I asked a question. "Do you have lawyers who can talk to his lawyers and explain how Randall is hurting himself and you by his behavior?"

"Been there, done that. Tried two different law firms even. Having failed miserably when I tried to put Uncle Randall under some kind of official supervision, he's deemed competent to conduct his own affairs."

"But his affairs are your affairs," Henny argued.

Daria shrugged. "The law says he's competent. I don't know what to do."

"Henny and I will look into this, I promise you," I said.

"I know you will," Daria said, rising. Henny popped up with her. "My head is pounding. I'm going home to rest." To Henny she said, "I'll call you when I'm feeling better."

"And I'll call you," Henny promised, "when Lloyd and I have any news." I noted his using the word "when" rather than "if." He went for her coat, then helped her into it.

"I'm so glad I met you, Henny," Daria said. The hug she gave him now had considerably more energy to it than her entry hug. "Thank you." She dove in and pecked Henny's lips. A moment later she was gone.

Henny stood, his back to me, studying the closed office door, his hand still holding the doorknob.

"Henny?"

"Yeah?" He released the doorknob and walked slowly back to this desk. "She wouldn't kiss me on Sunday night. Said she wanted to be certain I had proper respect for her. She kissed me now. Did you see?"

"I saw. She seems to have a bit of a high school mentality when it comes to... shall we call it... intimacy?"

"I don't know what she has, but I like it." He dropped into his chair. "What can we do about this uncle?"

"Good question," I muttered. The sound of the elevator had stopped, but then started right up again. "Someone coming up?" I asked.

Henny didn't respond so I went to the door. When the elevator stopped, I opened the door and stepped into the hallway. I saw a man coming our way. His face looked rigid, his jaw firmly set, his eyes on high beams, staring ahead. He stopped in front of me and looked at the writing on our door window.

"Henny and Lloyd's, right?" he asked.

"Yes. Would you like to come in?"

"You bet your ass I'd like to come in." And in he came. He stopped in front of Henny's desk and glanced at each of us. "Who's who?"

Henny answered for us and added, "Please, sit. What is your name?"

"Beckman. Paul Beckman."

While Henny circled his desk, I said, "Yes, Mr. Beckman. Detective Thursday told us you might be coming in. Uh, may I offer Henny's and my condolences—"

"Thank you, thank you. But I'm here for more than that. I want you two to find who did this to my daughter..."

Beckman needed a moment. He was a big man, taller than both Henny and me. I put him at about six-foot-two. He looked maybe fifty, not much more, and he had muscular arms. He'd handed his overcoat to Henny upon entering, and the tight sweater he wore let the world know he had some serious biceps. He still had his hair, dark and straight, with the beginnings of gray at the temples, combed straight back.

"I take it you're not satisfied with the police," I said.

Beckman pulled in two deep breaths before answering. "It's not that. I want the SOB who did this caught. The more people chasing him, the better."

Henny said, "Him? Do you suspect someone specific?"

"No, no. But I can't imagine another woman doing..."

He needed a moment again. Perhaps some refreshment, I thought. "Can I offer you coffee? Water? Even some whiskey."

"Whiskey, yes. Just a short one to settle me down."

I offered a warning. "It's likely a whiskey you've never tried."

"I don't care as long as it's whiskey."

Henny withdrew our *Boone's That's All* from his bottom drawer, while I got a coffee cup. Henny poured an inch into the cup, and I handed it to Beckman, who tossed it back cleanly. Definitely not his first rodeo.

"Good lord," he cried, smacking his lips together. "What is that? It's got some kick."

Henny lifted the bottle and displayed the label.

"I'll remember it. A little water, please?"

I complied and we three settled in again. An awkward moment of quiet descended on us, so I ventured, "How exactly would you like us to proceed?"

"You know how I'd like you to proceed! Find the person... Find the person."

Henny said, "The police have more machinery for doing that. I don't want to get your hopes up regarding what Lloyd and I can do."

I felt Henny was being a little too honest, but that's Henny. We had nothing on at the moment—I didn't count Uncle Randall as anything—plus a paying client was a paying client.

"Do you want me to leave then?" Beckman growled, rising.

"No, no," I said. "Sit, please. Henny and I are at your service, of course." As Beckman sat back down, I shot Henny a "shut-up" look.

Beckman had a checkbook in his hand. "The police recommended you. I want your help. Will two thousand be enough to get you started?"

"Sure," I answered. Beckman wrote and handed the check to Henny, who slid it into his top drawer. "Now, tell us everything you know."

"Nancy'd had her own apartment for a couple years. She was only twenty-four. Not too far from here. Henry Street. Decent neighborhood. Her building is across from a nice-looking public school. She worked in an insurance office. Not a top job, but she sounded content whenever I spoke with her. She's all I have...had. My wife passed away three years ago. Nancy and I spoke or texted nearly every day." Beckman's voice had dropped into a low, sad monotone. "Now, I don't know..." After taking a deep breath he went on. "Her office called me. She hadn't been at work and hadn't called in. I'd texted her as usual, but often she didn't respond right away. After the call from her office, I phoned her. No answer. I let one day go by, still with no response, so I made the trip in from New Jersey. Jersey City. I have a key to her place. I knocked but naturally, no answer. I went in." He lowered his eyes.

"And you called the police," I continued for him.

"Of course. I knew an ambulance wasn't needed. It was awful. Seeing her..." He shook his head and set his jaw.

"Had she been seeing anyone?" Henny asked, back on track, much to my relief.

"As in dating?"

"Yes."

"I think so. She mentioned a few times to me she'd been seeing someone, and she was really coming out of her shell. She was always a shy and quiet girl. She laughed when she told me. She never did explain what was so funny. She did tell me, though, she'd probably be letting this fellow go very soon. Again, laughing about it. I didn't get it then and I don't get it now, but I didn't want to pry. She's always been a sensible girl, and I trusted her judgment."

"Did she have any close friends you know of here in the city?" I asked. "Anyone she might have confided in?"

"A couple I know of and even met. Winnie Chu and Maria Cruz. I can text you their phone numbers. Hold on."

When he completed his texting, I asked, "Do you have access to her apartment now?"

"I still have the key. The police have been through the place. I suppose I have to clear out her things..."

He broke down again. Henny took out the Boone's again and held the bottle up.

Beckman waved his right hand as if he were saying goodbye. "No, no. I'm good. One of those is enough. Just give me a minute."

While Beckman put himself to rights, I spoke softly to Henny. "Shall we go take a look at the apartment?"

"No reason not to. It might..."

Henny's eyes popped and startled me. "What?" I asked him.

Henny whispered to me, "Henry Street! Randall Givens mentioned that street. The drop off."

"Right. The threatening note he found."

"Let's get a careful timeline on Nancy Beckman," Henny suggested.

I nodded. Maybe Henny had pulled a Sherlock Holmes moment out of the air—or in Henny's case, a Sam Spade moment.

Six

We, along with Beckman, took a cab to his daughter's building on Henry Street, a block lined with mostly six-story buildings of brick or brownstone across from a much more modern school. Beckman led us inside the building, then up a stairway to the third floor. His daughter's apartment lay at the end of the narrow hallway. I saw the bloodstain as soon as I entered, a dark splotch which had seeped into the corner of an area rug under a glass coffee table. I glanced at Beckman, but he appeared to be holding up. A litter of what appeared to be broken green and brown ceramics covered the immediate area. I presumed whatever Nancy Beckman had been struck with shattered on impact. A queasy wave traveled through my middle but, thankfully, didn't linger.

"This is where it happened," Beckman said, keeping eyes averted from the actual place where it happened. "She had the apartment fixed up real nice, don't you think?"

"Yes," Henny responded. "Much nicer than where I live. Lloyd and I each have an apartment in the same building in Williamsburg, just across the bridge. This is much homier."

"Way more cheerful," I added. "The police must have taken your daughter's cell phone?"

"No. Oddly enough, her phone was missing from the apartment, as well as her computer," Beckman explained.

Henny said, "That can only mean that the person who did this was somewhere on that phone and computer. Calls and texts and emails."

"That's what the police thought," Beckman said.

"When we find the guy, *his* phone will likely be evidence," Henny concluded.

I thought I'd check my ceramics assumption. "Mr. Beckman, what do you make of the broken pieces? A vase? Some kind of statue?"

"No, I don't think so. The last time I was here, oh, maybe a month ago, she had a number of little animals of those colors. If you're thinking they are part what..." Beckman had to stop.

To move the conversation forward but away from whatever had struck Nancy down, I said, "She collected these figurines, did she?"

Before Beckman could answer, Henny asked, "The police, I'm sure, looked over this place carefully. No photos of consequence, clothing left behind, nothing that could put another identifiable person in the apartment?"

Beckman shrugged. "I imagine they know their business, as far as it goes, but they have responsibilities other than finding out who did this to my daughter. It's why I've hired both of you."

Henny nodded.

The animal figurines thing still bothered me. "Why would her animal collection be destroyed like this?" I asked.

"Beats me. Someone hated turtles, I guess."

"I'm sorry?"

"This mess came from small green and brown replicas of turtles. I don't know where her interest in turtles came from."

Henny and I shared a glance.

"And she never mentioned where the turtles came from?" I asked.

"She said someone gave them to her. I found her tone to be very dismissive, but as I said, I don't like to pry."

"Only turtles?" I asked. "No other animals?"

"I only noticed turtles. I didn't linger over the collection, though," Beckman responded.

"How many of these turtles were there?" Henny asked.

"See that shelf?" Beckman indicated a short, empty shelf in an otherwise book-filled bookcase. "They were lined up there. Six or eight of them. I didn't count. Maybe a dozen. Do they mean anything?"

"No," I said quickly. "Just curious about why they were smashed."

"Take your time and go over the apartment, if you'd like," Beckman said. He sat on a chair, his back to the spot of the murder. Henny and I looked the apartment over, but I couldn't find anything worth commenting on, and neither could Henny.

"Thanks for allowing us in here," Henny said.

"Can I drop you somewhere?" Beckman asked.

"No, but thanks," I said. "It's getting late. Henny and I will head back to Brooklyn. If we find out anything, or need your help with something, we'll be certain to contact you."

Beckman led us outside, where we parted. Henny and I walked to the F train and went home.

By the time we got back to our apartments, we each had a self-assigned chore. Mine was to come up with a timeline for things from the moment Randall Givens walked into our office. Henny's was to get in touch with Detective Thursday and let him know about Randall's mysterious letter and coincidental drop-off of a mysterious passenger on Henry Street across from a school.

Over a glass of red wine, my list took no more than fifteen minutes to complete. My glass of wine wasn't half gone when I finished. Uncle Randall had shown up in our office the previous Tuesday. It was now late the following Monday. One week had elapsed. Daria's visit, her party, Susan's interviews, and our current day's afternoon with Paul Beckman were duly noted. I even listed the hours of the day the things occurred. Feeling quite satisfied with myself, I went to refill my wineglass, but my cell phone chimed. It was Henny.

"Thursday plans to send out a car to pick up Randall Givens. He wants to talk to him."

"I imagine he would. Does Thursday have any interest in turtles?"

"I mentioned Givens's turtles and the broken bric-a-brac, but he didn't display any particular interest. He did promise to get back to me after he spoke with Givens, though."

"So where does that leave us?" I asked.

"I guess it leaves us with talking Givens out of plopping down a few million dollars on a Baltimore turtle habitat. And it would be helpful if we can figure out who Nancy Beckman's final visitor was."

"I think I'd rather stay where I am for the time being and drink my wine."

"You got enough for two? I'll come up and we can discuss the case... cases."

"Sure. *In vino veritas.*"

"In where? What?"

"Never mind. Come on up."

As Henny and I got deeper into the case—and into the bottle(s) of wine, the more it appeared that Randall Givens' urge to perform a civic duty by visiting us had merit to it. But then there were the smashed turtles in the girl's apartment. What a coincidence, and I mean that ironically. I'd started wishing that turtles had gone the way of the Stegosaurus.

My cell made its noise, and I was surprised, no, shocked to hear someone on the other end shouting at me. From where Henny sat nearby, he could hear the turmoil coming out of my phone. I did what I could to calm my caller.

"Whoa, slow down. Who is this? Please, settle down; take it easy." I held the phone, still spewing high decibels of reproach, away from me and to Henny I whispered, "Paul Beckman."

"What's got him so bent out of shape?"

I gave Henny a 'come-on-make-a-guess' look.

"Yeah, I know, but something's really set him off." He gestured toward my phone.

I nodded and frowned. "Sir, is this Mr. Beckman? Tell me what's wrong. Yes, my partner and I were sitting here discussing your case." I listened, barely able to get a word in, but I agreed with everything he said, and little by little, his decibel level sank back to socially appropriate. I gave him a few more words of agreement and an assurance that Henny and I were on the job. I ended the call with him on a cautionary note. When he finally hung up, I sank back on my sofa. "Henny, that man has forced me back into sobriety."

"Damn him. What got him going?"

"Seems like he spends a lot of his time in the police station. Thursday assured him he had a lead and would bring Randall Givens in to discuss his passenger and the note. Seems they haven't located Givens yet, though. That's what's got Beckman up in arms."

"What was your 'I wouldn't do that if I were you' about?"

"He said he knew where Givens lived—he said he noticed the address on a paper on Thursday's desk when the detective stepped out of the room for a moment—and he would visit him himself."

"Geez, what could go wrong?"

"Everything."

"You think you convinced him to let Thursday and the police—and me and you—work on things and he should stay out of it himself?"

"Well, he did say I was probably right—about him not visiting Givens."

"Only 'probably?'"

I shrugged.

"Let's go into the office early tomorrow," Henny said. "And give Susan a call tonight and fill her in."

Henny returned to his own apartment, and I made myself something to eat. Afterward, I spoke with Susan for some forty minutes before turning in for the night.

Seven

The next morning Henny and I sat sipping coffee and sharing the four donuts he'd generously brought to the office, bought at a bakery he sometimes stopped at a block from us.

I thanked him, then said, "Guess what Susan told me last night. By the way, have you talked to Daria lately?"

"Sure. I check in with her every day, but she's always so busy, the conversations are usually short."

"Did Daria mention anything about a trip to Atlantic City?"

"A couple times, yeah. She said hiring a cook for our get together was a lot of bother."

"She's already called Susan and invited her—and, of course, me—along to an Atlantic City jaunt."

"Yeah, she mentioned doing that. Are you coming?"

I laughed. "Would you prefer Susan and I go to Schenectady instead?"

"No, no. I'm happy Daria seems set on joining our threesome."

"And you're intent on you and she becoming a twosome."

Henny smiled. "I like her."

I nodded. "There's a lot there to like."

"She and I are going to Giandos tonight." Henny shot me a wary glance. "The two of us."

"Nice. I won't interfere. If the Atlantic City excursion comes up in conversation, you can tell Daria Susan and I are in."

"I will." Henny paused for a moment. "It's likely each couple will have its own room, eh? You think so, right?"

"More likely, one double and two singles."

"Shut up."

I laughed and we returned to our doughnuts. When they were gone, Henny called Detective Thursday, who reported that he still not been able to get in touch with Randall Givens. Henny passed along Daria Givens' cell number, suggesting she might know where to find her uncle. Thursday called back fifteen minutes later and told us that Daria believed her uncle had gone to Baltimore for a day or two. Henny explained about the turtle conservatory. Thursday's reply was not for a general audience, and even though Henny was not on speakerphone, I could hear the word "turtles" repeated a few times preceded by a certain spicy adjective.

Henny put the phone down after he ended the call and blew on his fingers.

"Thursday's hot, eh?" I said, grinning.

"Yes, but he said he'll keep checking and have Uncle Randall picked up as soon as he returns to his apartment. They definitely want to talk to him."

My cell rang and I frowned at Henny. "Beckman."

"Good morning, Mr. Beckman," I greeted, and he launched into a diatribe about the NYPD and how they couldn't find an apple in an apple orchard, and did we know about the drop-off of the hitchhiker and the threatening letter? I didn't think it wise to admit Henny's and my being the source of that information, not with

Beckman in his current irate condition. I promised him that Henny and I would keep in close touch with Detective Thursday, and, in fact, had just spoken with him, and would pass along any information we picked up. He again mentioned interviewing Randall Givens on his own, and again, I discouraged him.

"When are we going to Atlantic City?" I asked Henny when I finished with Beckman. "I could use the break."

"Let me call Daria," Henny said.

Henny's call resulted in Daria's promise to clear her busy schedule for an overnight trip to Ocean Casino, leaving NYC tomorrow morning and returning the next day, Thursday, in the early afternoon. I was tasked with having Susan in our office at ten a.m., where Daria would meet us in the limousine she'd rent.

"So, what do we do until then?" I asked my partner. "We've got a whole day ahead of us."

"Why don't we find those two friends of Nancy Beckman and talk to them?"

"Yeah, good idea. Make the calls."

Henny made the calls, and we were off—a noon appointment with Winnie Chu and a two o'clock appointment with Maria Cruz.

~ * ~

Winnie Chu worked in the Citibank branch at the foot of Mott Street. We found her at the welcome desk, and after a word with her supervisor, she led us down a flight of stairs into a small conference room.

"I can give you maybe fifteen minutes. My boss is covering for me." Winnie smiled. "You can guess how much she likes doing that. But she's nice." Winnie looked to be in her early twenties and dressed professionally. I noticed Henny's gaze gravitate to the small diamond ring on her left hand, so I figured he'd be all business in the interview. Besides, there was Daria to consider.

Henny took the lead. "We're sorry about your friend, Nancy." Winnie's smile disappeared.

"Yes, I can't believe it. She was a really good friend."

"Can you tell me whether she was seeing anyone?"

"Oh sure. Nancy was popular and had no trouble meeting people. My fiancé and I doubled-dated with her lots of times."

Henny nodded. "Who was she seeing lately?"

Winnie heaved a sigh. "She was kind of mysterious about him. I don't know why. She said he was very generous with her but was kind of freaky."

"Freaky how?" I asked.

"He kept pets, she said."

"Did she mention the kind of pets?"

"No. Like I said, she was mysterious about him. I never got to meet him."

Henny asked, "Did she ever mention a young man whom she might have ditched lately? Someone who might have been the type to hitchhike long distances, like up the Jersey Turnpike carrying a duffel bag?"

The look on Winnie's face changed to one of incredulity. "No. Hitchhike? No. I met the two fellows she dated previous to the mysterious fellow. They were both solid citizens. I can't see them hitchhiking with a duffel bag on their shoulders."

I looked at my watch and said, "We'll try not to keep you. Did she seem, you know, head over heels with the man who had pets, or did she indicate that perhaps she'd had enough of him."

"Nancy told me she was ready for our double dating again. I asked if we'd finally get to meet the mystery man. She laughed and said no. She said enough was enough."

"What did she mean by that?" Henny asked.

"She made a passing comment I didn't follow up on. Something about him wanting her to take care of his pets. Her tone made me think the possibility of that was zero."

"I see," Henny said softly. "Lloyd?"

"I think you've given us some help, Ms. Chu."

"I hope I have. Nancy deserves justice. She was a good friend and a nice person."

Henny and I rose, and Henny gestured Winnie to precede us up the stairs. We thanked her again, and she said we could contact her any time if it would help.

Outside, Henny and I crossed Chatham Square toward Dim Sum Go Go.

"What do you think?" I asked.

"Turtles smashed in the girl's apartment. Gifts from Randall? Taking care of his pets—turtles? Her desire not to publicize their relationship. His freakiness—his turtles... and him? She liked getting stuff from him and being taken places, maybe. Expensive places she may never have been, but she drew the line at turtle-sitting."

"We can't be certain, but it sounds like Randall. How could it be anyone else? What was with Randall's hitchhiker story, though?"

Henny shrugged. "Maybe he thought it gave him a great alibi."

"He's nuts if he thought that. It puts him right in the neighborhood."

"Daria claims he's nuts." Henny checked his watch. "Call Maria Cruz. See if she can meet us a little earlier. Maybe one or one-thirty."

I made the call, but Maria assured me that two o'clock was the only time she could abandon the desk at the tennis club where she worked welcoming players and conducting business, so Henny and I dawdled over our Dim Sum Go Go lunch and afterward made our slow way to Long Island City, where the club was located a short distance from the Midtown Tunnel.

Henny and I splurged on a taxi to get there.

Maria was a tall young woman with a bright smile and long, brown hair. Henny and I introduced ourselves, and five minutes later, the three of us were off in a corner of the players' lounge conversing in soft voices. We offered our condolences over the loss of her friend and asked pretty much the same questions we'd directed at Winnie Chu. We managed to extract one additional piece of information Winnie hadn't provided.

"Yes, Nancy said he was kind of weird and older than she was. But she liked how much money he spent on her. He liked buying her things."

I asked, "Is that the kind of girl Nancy was? Eager to take advantage?"

"No, not at all," Maria retorted. She seemed offended by the suggestion. "Never. No. It seemed like a joke to her, and if it was a joke to her, how could it be a serious thing? It struck me that each of them realized their running together was a passing flirtation. At least that's the impression I got from Nancy's attitude and comments."

"She never told you his name?" Henny asked.

"No, she kept him under an air of mystery. I said that to her once, and she laughed. 'My man of mystery' she called him from then on."

"Did you get the sense she was finished with him?"

"Yes, I did. Come, I'll show you why I say that."

Maria led us back to the front desk. She pointed and there, on a shelf against the mirrored rear of the space, sat three small, deep green, ceramic turtles.

Henny and I exchanged glances.

"What are we to understand by that?" I asked.

"Nancy told me she was sick of these little turtle things he kept giving her. I remember her saying, 'This has to stop.' She gave me these. I didn't want them in my apartment, so I brought them here."

"Did Nancy mention anything about him having pets?"

"No. I think she was embarrassed by him, if you really want to know. I never got to meet him. She didn't much want to talk about him. She did seem over him because she promised we'd be going out together again soon. By us I mean Nancy and a date and me and my husband. I knew she didn't mean with the mystery guy."

We thanked Maria, who directed us to the nearest subway, and an hour later, Henny and I were back in our office, pondering.

I insisted on our telling Detective Thursday what we'd learned from Nancy Beckman's two friends. "He'll need that information if he ever gets to interview Uncle Randall."

"He's gotta have the names of the two women we just spoke to."

"We don't know that."

"We got the names from Beckman. Thursday has spoken to Beckman, and Beckman wouldn't let any information that could help the police go unsaid."

Henny had a point. "I guess so. It couldn't hurt, though, talking to Thursday. He may have news for us, too."

Henny still acted uncertain.

"You're not worried about Daria reacting negatively to any of this, are you. I know she wants her uncle acting with restraint, but if he really is the mysterious boyfriend..."

"I know. I know." Henny rubbed his hands up and down his face.

"Make the call," I urged.

Henny heaved a sigh and rang up the detective. He went through our two interviews, and we waited for Thursday's reaction.

"Givens still isn't home," Thursday said. "I told you. His niece says he's probably in Baltimore, but I have a car stop by his place every couple hours. The niece gave me his cell number, but he doesn't answer."

"If the caller ID shows up NYPD, no wonder he doesn't answer," I said, leaning toward Henny's phone.

"I left a message about his report to you about the hitchhiker. He has no reason to think it's about anything other than that," Thursday argued.

"Yeah, probably," I agreed. "Is our client leaving you alone?"

"Who? The girl's father. Jeez, he's here every day—more than once— asking questions, making suggestions, spouting off. He doesn't think we're doing enough. I'd like to toss him in the cooler for some peace and quiet. Look, I'm glad you told me about those two women, the dead girl's friends. Beckman gave me their names, but I hadn't gotten to them yet. I'll bring them in. Yeah, he gave me their phone numbers. I'll do it right now. Thanks for the call."

"Keep us informed," Henny said.

"Will do." Half an hour later, Henny left the office early to go home and get himself ready for his dinner with Daria and our imminent trip to Atlantic City.

Eight

Daria and the limo showed up on time, and we had a pleasant drive down the Garden State Parkway to the Atlantic City Expressway and into AC. I had to contain myself when Daria checked us in and handed one key card to me, then turned, handed another key card to Henny, and said, "Here. You'll like our room." Henny tried acting so cool, but I knew he was on the verge of needing CPR. I had no trouble believing Henny would like their room.

Susan's and my room was spectacular. The windows looked north and east, out toward the ocean and overlooking Brigantine, the next town north. We gathered for lunch at Noodles of the World, just off the casino floor, and after lunch, Daria led us out into the casino proper. It being a Wednesday afternoon, it wasn't crowded.

"I'm going to do some gambling," she announced cheerily. "You don't want to go where I'm going. In fact, they wouldn't even let you in."

"Why not? Where are you going?" Henny asked, a puzzled look on his face.

"High limit slots. You can't get into the room without one of these." She withdrew a black, what looked like, credit card from her tiny purse. "Fancy member's card," she explained with a quick laugh. "Why don't you do a little gambling yourself? You never know." She pecked Henny's cheek and walked off. We watched her approach a large room on the edge of the gambling floor and, after flashing her black card and having a quick chat and friendly laugh with a guard stationed outside the room, she went inside.

"So, what do we do beside wait for a nifty dinner?" I asked.

Susan answered, "I'm going to browse the retail shops. I'm sure they have some nice things. The question will be, can I afford any of the nice things?" Aping Daria's insouciant departure, she said, "Good luck. You never know," gave a quick laugh, and walked off.

Henny and I stared at each other.

"You gambling?" I asked.

"I've only been in a casino twice. I only know how to do slot machines. Anything with lots of rules..." He shook his head.

I laughed. "I'll keep you company. I'm not a gambler, myself."

"I hear they have penny machines. Can't lose much on a penny machine," Henny said.

"We'll see." We found a machine with a 1-cent sign on it, and Henny slid a twenty into the maw of the beast.

"Twenty bucks—that's two thousand chances."

Henny studied the face of the machine intently.

"What's the problem?" I asked.

He stabbed a line of text with his index finger. I leaned closer to inspect it.

"Seventy-five cent minimum bet," I read aloud.

"How is this a penny machine if you have to bet seventy-five cents?" Henny asked.

"I guess it's a seventy-five-penny machine."

"What the hell? False advertising."

"In for a penny..." I said.

Henny glared at me. "You think you're funny."

"Take a shot. You never know."

"Oh, look. What a break! It says I can double or even triple my bet."

"The more you bet, the more you can win," I encouraged.

"You're a big help. Why don't you get a job with gamblers' anonymous?"

"They probably pay about as much as these machines do. Not very well."

"You should do stand-up," Henny grumbled.

"Come on. Take a shot. Twenty bucks gives you about twenty-five chances."

With a shake of his head, Henny pushed the Bet 1 button. The machine went through its noises and cartoon display and...WINNER.

"Hey, you won!" I cried, genuinely excited for my pal. "What did you win?"

"It says I won thirty cents."

"There you go. Thirty cents to the good."

"But I bet seventy-five cents."

We were quiet for a moment before I said, "The machine should've said LOSER... of forty-five cents."

Henny struck the BET 1 button a bit harder than before. WINNER!

"Another winner," I cried. "How much did you lose this time?"

"I won fifteen cents," he muttered.

"So down another sixty cents. This is nuts."

Henny managed about thirty punches of the BET 1 button and won twenty-two times. Then he was out of money.

He got up from his seat in front of the slot machine. "I'm done with that. Gambling is for morons," he said. Suddenly, a bell rang repeatedly. Two rows over, an older woman with white hair sat smiling and being congratulated by three other older women with equally white hair. I walked over and saw on the screen of her slot machine, WINNER $125.00. I reported the miracle to Henny.

"Great," he said disgustedly. "I guarantee you I won't be back in front of one of these machines until I have a head of hair as white as Miss Lucky Winner there."

I laughed and said, "Let's go browse the retail stores. If it's not too cold outside, we can take a walk on the boardwalk. And don't be depressed. Remember, Daria reserved only two rooms." Henny finally smiled, and we left the casino floor.

~ * ~

We reconvened for dinner at Amada, an upscale, pricey casino restaurant where we enjoyed "Spanish ambiance with authentic Mediterranean details." And the food and wine were good, too. When the check came, Daria offered the waiter her magical black card as well as her driver's license.

"I pay with points," Daria explained with what seemed to me a nervous grin. "They already took enough of my money." She left a hundred-dollar bill for the waiter, and as we exited from the restaurant to the casino floor she said, "I'm going back to gamble some more. The tide has to turn. Good metaphor for Ocean Casino, eh?" She gave an uneasy laugh. To Henny she said, "I'll see you back in the room. Go and enjoy yourself."

"Well," Susan said, "the young lady does like to challenge the gods of chance."

"Henny, are you going back to the slots?" I asked.

He looked at me. "I'd sooner sit for a root canal. What'll we do?"

After some discussion, we decided to take the boardwalk to the next casino down, Hard Rock, and see what it had to offer. After admiring the rock and roll memorabilia there and having a drink, we returned to Ocean.

"Have a nice night," I teased Henny. He shot me a thumbs up and headed for the elevator.

Next morning, we four met for breakfast at a small food court type restaurant. Again, Daria paid with her points and then gave us a small jolt.

"I'm going to hang around here for another night. You three can go back to New York in the limousine. I'll manage." To Henny, she said, "Can we meet at your favorite restaurant Friday, say around seven?"

"Sure. You'll find me at the bar," Henny assured her. "Still hoping for your luck to change?"

I controlled my eyebrows and kept them from raising when Daria put her hand atop Henny's and said, "It already has."

"I'll be happy to stay with you," Henny offered. "Lloyd can handle the office."

Daria managed a weak grin and replied, "Thanks, but I'll be busy. I'll see you Friday around seven."

Daria went one way, and we rode up the elevator to gather our things, then made for the limousine. When we were settled in for the ride north, I asked, "How was your night, pal?"

Susan gave me a playful slap, and Henny simply smiled and said, "Very pleasant."

After an hour's drive up the Garden State Parkway, my cell rang. I checked the screen. "Mr. Beckman," I told Henny.

"Better take it," he said.

I hit speakerphone and Beckman's voice came in loud and clear. "Something's going on. Something happened and Detective Thursday seems much more eager to find Randall Givens."

"He still isn't back from Baltimore?"

"No, but they've phoned and visited his apartment. A young woman was there twice when they visited, but she didn't know when he'd be back. Tell me. Is he the guy? Did he kill my daughter?"

Henny's eyes met mine. I felt Susan's hand grip mine. "No," I said. "I can't tell you he is."

"What can you tell me? Don't put me off. If he's the guy, I want to know."

"I know there are some questions he needs to answer, but I can't say what the outcome of that will be or whether his answers will solve anything. But trust me. Detective Thursday will get the truth out of him, and you should leave things to him."

"I get the feeling the detective is pretty sure he's the guy. I sense it when he tries to put me off."

"Henny and I would likely know about it if it were true. My advice to you is to let it play out. Givens can't stay away from home forever. Henny and I will be in close touch with Detective Thursday, and, of course, the moment we learn anything of substance, we'll be in touch with you."

Without a farewell, Beckman ended the call. I was glad we were only an hour or so away from home.

The limo driver dropped us off on Centre Street in front of our building. After a hurried conference in the backseat, which had begun as we exited the Holland Tunnel, we offered the driver a hundred-dollar tip, basing our generosity on what we'd seen Daria do for the waiter at Amada the previous evening, and sent him away happy. Henny went for some pizza while Susan and I took our rickety elevator to the office.

"Well, that was fun," Susan announced, setting down her small suitcase and taking our client chair.

"Yeah, it was," I agreed. "Nice to get a change like that and good restaurant food with so little damage to the bank account."

Susan laughed. "Daria doesn't appear to concern herself with gambling losses."

"How do you know she had losses?"

"Lloyd, really? Her attitude and mood and refusing to forgo the fancy slot room after dinner and staying on today? She lost and wanted to recoup. And the points on her black card. The more and the longer you gamble, the more points you accumulate, and she had a barrelful of points to pay for the couple of meals we had."

"I guess. I wonder if Uncle Randall knows she's such a gambler."

"That reminds me. Let me give Detective Thursday a call," Susan said. "Maybe something broke while we were coming home."

"Go ahead." I went to our mini-fridge and took out two bottles of water. I opened one for Susan and set it on the edge of my desk.

She asked for Thursday, and after a brief conversation said, "Randall Givens finally responded to Thursday's search party. He'll be back on Eleventh Street sometime today."

I thought for a moment. "I feel guilty about ditching Beckman's case for the day in AC. I'll call him and let him know the interview with Givens will likely take place today."

I made the call and Beckman sounded properly grateful. Henny arrived with a half a pizza in tow. Henny and Susan split the fourth piece. We filled Henny in on the new development.

"Will Thursday call us after the interview?" he asked, lifting a dangle of cheese from his chin.

"He said he'd keep me up-to-date, and I should pass anything he tells me on to you," Susan said.

The pizza gone, Susan went back to her office, and Henny and I settled in for the afternoon.

Nine

The afternoon remained quiet as did most of the evening. I lay on my sofa watching an old Jeremy Brett-Sherlock Holmes tale when my cell chimed. The caller ID informed me that Paul Beckman wanted to talk. I didn't much feel like adding him to my evening, but I still felt guilty about abandoning him for Atlantic City, so I answered.

"Mr. Beckman, hello. What's up?"

"I've been arrested is what's up."

"What! Why?"

"Randall Givens is dead. Murdered, your police detective tells me. And they think I did it because his girlfriend says she saw me go into his apartment tonight."

"What! What else did she say? Did she see anyone other than you going inside? And did you go inside?"

"Yes, yes. I was there. I heard at the police station Givens had finally returned, and I knew where he lived. I wanted to talk to him before the police picked him up. He let me in and gave me the same story he told you about dropping off a hitchhiker and seeing him enter my daughter's building and the crazy letter he claims to have found."

"Did the girlfriend see you leave?"

"I don't know, but she's nuts if she thinks I went in there to kill the man. When I saw he wasn't about to deviate from his story, I left. I didn't want to complicate things by having to explain my presence to the police if they showed up. Now, Detective Thursday let me call you. I don't know what to do."

"Okay, listen. I'll have Henny call the detective and see if he'll share the girlfriend's contact information with us. We'll talk to her. You'll probably need a lawyer. Henny and I know a couple dependable ones. Sit tight and we'll be in touch."

"Sit tight! What the hell else am I supposed to do?"

I called Henny and filled him in. He called back fifteen minutes later to tell me he'd already made a call to Ginger Gadsman, Randall's girlfriend, and we had an appointment with her tomorrow morning at ten in our office.

~ * ~

Ginger proved to be a young woman with faintly red hair. Henny ushered her to our client chair, placed midway between Henny's and my desks.

"Thanks for coming in to talk to us," I said, after offering her water or coffee, both of which she declined.

"I never want an experience like yesterday's again ever. It was horrible."

"Tell us what happened," Henny said.

"I was going to Randall's, but I saw this man at his door. Randall's on the first floor, and I watched the man go inside the building, and through the windows I saw him enter Randall's apartment."

"You're certain he went into Mr. Givens' apartment?" I asked.

"Yes. I saw the two of them together through the windows. I told you it's on the first floor and faces Eleventh Street. Anyone could see in."

"How long did the man stay?"

"I thought he might be one of the lawyers Randall is using to take care of his turtle project. He was a wonderful man, the way he took care of his turtles."

"The turtle project was the Baltimore thing?" Henny asked.

"Yes. I didn't want to be in the way, so I went for a walk along Fourteenth Street and window shopped."

"How long before you returned to Mr. Givens' place?"

"Not real long. Forty minutes the most."

"And..." Henny urged.

"And I have my own key. I looked through the living room windows—I told you they're right on street level—and didn't see the two men, so I presumed the lawyer—I thought he was a lawyer—had left. I went inside and there was Randall on the floor with a bloody head. It was awful."

Henny and I gave Ginger a moment to gather herself. When she calmed down, I asked, "Did you see anyone else near the apartment? Going in or out?"

"No, no one. I phoned the police right away. Something made them suspect... what did they say his name was?"

"Paul Beckman," I answered. "His daughter was recently murdered, and Mr. Givens had some information that could be pertinent. Did Givens mention anything to you about his picking up a passenger on his way home from Baltimore recently?"

"No, no he didn't." Ginger's brow furrowed. "He usually tells me everything. But when the police showed me a picture of Beckman, I recognized him as the man who went into the apartment."

Henny spoke up. "We don't think Mr. Beckman did this to Mr. Givens, and we're going to try to find out who did. We *were* trying to find out who killed Mr. Beckman's daughter. Now, this has been added to the pot."

"Well, I hope you do. Randall lying there... it was awful, just terrible." Ginger got to her feet. "I hope I've helped you some. Please let me know if I can help some more."

"You've helped us a great deal," I complimented and received a quick smile in return. Ginger left us and Henny and I mulled things over.

"No way Beckman bashed in Givens' head," Henny said. "He *might* be capable of doing it, but not if he wasn't certain Givens was the killer."

"I think you're right. And who would blame him? But not like this, not when he couldn't be sure."

"I wonder if Daria knows about her uncle," Henny said. "I guess I should call her."

"Thursday likely already saw to that."

"Yeah, but if he didn't, she needs to know. I don't want her angry at me for not telling her. I didn't call her last night. I didn't want to interrupt her slot playing."

"She'll forgive you. Let her know we interviewed Ginger today and are following up."

Henny made the call, but when Daria didn't pick up, I made a suggestion.

"Call Ocean. Maybe she hasn't checked out yet."

"I hope she's not planning on another night of slot machines. We're supposed to meet at Giandos tonight. Let me find the number for Ocean."

Henny made the call and explained the situation to the desk clerk. "Daria Givens is the name. She stayed Wednesday night, then extended her stay over Thursday night. I'd like you to ring her room if she hasn't checked out."

A furrow appeared between Henny's eyebrows. "Are you sure? That doesn't make any sense. Well, if you're certain... Bye."

"What?" I asked.

"She checked out yesterday, according to the guy I talked to."

"So, she should be at home. Call her again. If she doesn't pick up, we'll go to her place and knock on her door."

"Let me call Thursday first and ask if she's been told her uncle's been killed."

Henny made another call. When he finished, he said, "They haven't been able to reach her either."

"The Givens family is proving very elusive. Try her again."

When this call failed, we made the twenty-minute walk to Nassau Street and rang her buzzer. Still nothing.

Henny said, "Should I tell her by text her uncle's dead? That seems a little cold."

"Tell her you have news she needs to know, and she should get in touch with you immediately. Otherwise, you'll see her at Giandos as scheduled tonight."

Henny agreed it was all he could do, so he did it, and as we went back to our office, a thought struck me.

"Henny, it doesn't make sense she checked out on Thursday. Checkout time is something like eleven o'clock. We left in her limo around ten. I guess she could have paid for the room and checked out whenever she wanted to on Thursday. Still, it doesn't make sense."

"Yeah, and...?"

"She'd certainly come home by limo. I don't see her taking a bus."

"No. Knowing her as I do, I can confirm, she would *not* take a bus. And so?"

"Call the limo company, say you work for her, and she thinks she may have left her purse or something in the car. And find out what time she took the ride north. This is getting a little too *noir* for me."

I could tell Henny didn't like his forties' fetish turned against us. He frowned and said, "All of a sudden I'm feeling leery about tonight's dinner with her."

"Here, I took one of the limo company's cards. When we get back to the office, make the call."

I dug into my wallet and handed the card to Henny. Then, we walked back to Centre Street in silence.

When we entered our office, Henny slung his fedora at the coat stand. It missed the prongs, bounced off the wall, and landed upside down on the floor.

"Figures," Henny grumbled as he retrieved the hat and hung it up. Once he was seated, he put the limo business card in front of him and punched in the number on his cell phone.

"Speaker," I reminded him.

"Hello. Golden Limousines."

"Yeah, my employer, Daria Givens, used your service yesterday and believes she may have left a small purse in the car. Did your driver turn anything in?"

"Daria Givens. Yes, a steady customer. Let me check." After a moment of silence, during which I whispered to Henny that he should ask what time the ride began, the voice on the phone returned. "It seems she must have lost her purse yesterday since she only left AC today about an hour ago."

Henny and I shared a puzzled look. Henny ran his tongue across his lips and said, "Yes, she told me when she noticed the purse was missing yesterday. What time was her ride yesterday?"

"Let's see. Thursday at eleven-fifteen. Same time as she left today... and I'm sorry. I don't see any report from yesterday's driver about anything being left behind in the car. Our drivers are required to check after every trip."

"I see. I'll tell Ms. Givens that. Thank you very much." The call ended.

I asked, "She made a trip yesterday and another trip today?"

Henny stared at the cell phone on his desk.

"Well," I prodded. "What do you think?"

"I don't know. I don't know."

"Let me, then. According to the fellow you just chatted with, Daria took a limo yesterday, an hour after we left Atlantic City. Somehow, she ended up back in Atlantic City and is coming home again today, right now, in fact. How can that be?"

"Maybe the guy made a mistake," Henny argued.

"I think you better give Detective Thursday a call. Let him dig into this. The limo people can blow us off, but they'll have to answer his questions. If we call back, they'll get suspicious and start blabbing about the confidentiality of their clients."

Henny heaved a sigh and looked my way.

I tried to encourage him. "You're probably right, though. Likely a mix-up in the limo records. It'll be better if it gets straightened out."

"Right," Henny mumbled. His cell chimed. He looked at it and said, "Daria!"

"Speaker," I snapped.

"Hi, Daria. What's up?"

"Hi, love. I'm on my way home and looking forward to seeing you tonight. We're still on, aren't we?"

"Of course. What did you do yesterday after we left?"

I thought it a bold question from Henny. I mouthed Uncle Randall to him.

"I gambled most of the day. Almost came out even for the trip." She added a little laugh. "Six o'clock tonight okay with you?"

"You bet, but there's something I'm afraid you don't know."

"What is it?"

"Your uncle Randall."

"Yes, what about him?"

"Uh, he's been murdered."

"What! What are you talking about?"

Henny provided what details we knew.

"Oh, my god," Daria muttered. "What should I do?"

"Well, I think you better check in with the police. They've been trying to contact you to let you know. I tried calling you, too."

"My phone's been off. This is awful."

"Let me give you the number of Detective Thursday. He's on the case."

"And they've arrested the killer?"

"Like I said, they think they have."

"Good. I hope he gets what he deserves. I can barely process this right now. I'll... I'll call this detective when I get home. I can't now. It's too much. We're nearly at the Holland Tunnel. And I really need to see you tonight. Oh, Henny..." We heard sniffling.

Henny said, "I'll be at Giandos waiting for you."

"Yes, yes. Thank you. I hope I'll be okay by then." After a prodigious sniff she said, "Bye, darling," and ended the call.

Henny tapped his fingers on the screen of his phone. "I should call Thursday."

"You should. He'll need to know all of this before Daria calls him. He'll get it straightened out. Probably an honest mistake somewhere. Don't worry."

"I'll be back in a minute." Henny rose and left the office. He turned left toward the restroom, but I figured he simply needed a few minutes alone. I felt sorry for him.

Ten

For the rest of the day, the unspeakable remained unsaid, as did most of anything else. Henny's call to Detective Thursday went off honestly and did little to lift his spirits. I wanted to call Susan and bring her up to date, but I couldn't bring myself to do it in front of Henny. If I left the office, I feared Henny would guess my purpose, which would only make things worse. He looked miserable enough, so miserable, in fact, that I refused to do anything to add to his fears. I was even afraid to suggest he go home early and get ready for his dinner with Daria. Finally, though, he had to leave. I wished him well, but at the office door, he turned to me and said, "Thursday wants me to keep her at Giandos as late as possible." He shrugged and closed the door behind him.

I didn't hear the elevator and presumed Henny had taken the stairs. I allowed him five minutes before placing my call to Susan. I gave her every detail I could, along with voicing the obvious suspicions.

"You really think she could have...?" Susan didn't complete the sentence. I gave her a few seconds, but she remained silent.

"You'll have a big story if she did."

"I'll stay in touch with Thursday. He likes seeing his name in the newspaper. I told you, we're good buddies by now. I'm certain he'll keep me in the loop."

Other than for some cookies that had languished in our minifrig, neither Henny nor I had much of an appetite that day, so, feeling blue myself, I walked the half hour to Chelsea and plopped myself down at the bar of Bocca di Bacca on the corner of Twentieth and Ninth. I had their wild mushroom bruschetta and three glasses of merlot. I desperately wished to be a fly on the wall at Giandos. However, I'd never seen a fly in Giandos. I splurged on a taxi back to Brooklyn and waited up for my friend.

I didn't hear anything from him that night and didn't have the nerve to call him. If he had any desire to share the details of his evening, I figured he'd ring me. I heard nothing from Susan either. I *knew* she'd call me, so I guessed that either nothing *had* happened or that something *was* happening, and she couldn't break away. So, I went to bed and slept poorly.

~ * ~

I didn't disturb Henny next morning and sat alone in my apartment until Susan texted she would be with me around eleven. When I let her in, her face told the story.

"You were right," she said. "She did it."

"Good lord. Do you know the details?"

"Yes. I've been up all night. I wanted to come see you and then go home and sleep."

"You don't have to go home to sleep, but let's hear."

"I got this all from Thursday."

"I'll bet he looks good in the telling."

Susan offered a smile. "He and two of his people were at Giandos' bar. He already had tracked Daria's movements the past couple days. She did take a limo right after we left, what, an hour or so later. Thursday filled Henny in on everything he learned, and the plan was for Henny to break it to her little by little as Thursday and his men watched her reaction."

"They treated Henny like a detective rather than a man smitten."

"It was hard for him. Have you heard from him yet?"

"Nope."

"He was still with Thursday when I left to come to you. Well, it turns out that Daria made a phone call to Uncle Randall's lawyers that morning, right after we left and hung up steaming mad, according to them. Also, Randall's girlfriend wasn't the only one who saw Paul Beckman go into Randall's apartment. Daria wanted to see her uncle, too, but she didn't go away when she saw Beckman go into the apartment. She hung around until he came out. Then she went in. According to the lawyers, she was crazy upset about Randall plunking down three point five million dollars for his turtle village. It would have cramped her style severely."

"Gambling?"

"Right. Thursday found out she spent a considerable amount of time... and money... in Ocean Casino. They liked having her visit and treated her well. You can guess why."

"She left a lot of money behind, no doubt."

"You're quite the detective." Susan smiled again, and I was glad, as always, that I'd met her. "We know what happened. She and Randall argued, and she left him there on the floor. The girlfriend was still walking along Fourteenth Street and never saw Daria."

"So, then Daria went back to Atlantic City?"

"Right away. By bus. Got a room at a motel and took the limo back the next day, imagining she'd never be suspected or questioned and if she was, she had the Friday limo receipt as an alibi. She thought she'd covered her tracks."

"Boy, was she ever wrong."

"She's in jail, and Paul Beckman is not. It's likely he'll call and be in to see you soon."

My cell chimed. To Susan I said, "It's Henny." I took a deep breath, connected, and listened, Susan's eyes fixed on me. "Sure," I responded. "Absolutely. Susan's here with me now. Okay." The call ended. "Henny's coming here, and he's bringing Paul Beckman with him. He claims to know what happened to Beckman's daughter."

Susan and I sat around and made what idle chatter we were capable of, Susan throwing in a prodigious yawn now and then. In time, we heard a knock, and I went to welcome Henny and Beckman.

"Have you been to bed?" I asked Henny. Beckman didn't look so good either.

"No. Worst night of my life."

Susan and I greeted Beckman and we sat, two on my sofa and two on random chairs.

An awkward pause ensued. Finally, Henny said, "Randall Givens was the guy."

Beckman covered his face with his hands. We maintained a sorrowful silence for him, but he recovered quickly and said, "Tell them. I can't." Beckman looked at me. "It's like you said."

"What was it I said?"

"You said the... the killer's phone held the story."

Henny took up the tale. "Mr. Beckman's daughter..."

"Nancy. Call her Nancy," Beckman insisted.

Henny obeyed. "Nancy and Givens were tight for a few months, but he was going off to Baltimore often and every time he did, he asked her to take care of his turtles. Feed them, whatever. Finally, she'd had enough. Angry texts went back and forth. His next to last text ordered—and 'ordered' is the right word—ordered her to visit his apartment every day he was away and tend to his turtles. She said she didn't want to. He repeated his demand, but Nancy didn't respond. When Givens got home... without having transported any mysterious hitchhiker to Henry Street and Nancy's building... he found five of his turtles dead and, it was clear to him that his turtles had gone unfed. We know this from his final text which gave a terrible earful to Nancy about losing his precious turtles and how could she do that... and his turtles deserved to live more than she did. It was ugly. He ended the text telling her he was coming over to talk to her."

A tearful Beckman interrupted. "Why didn't she get out? Why didn't she simply leave or call the police or call me? Why?" He heaved a deep sigh. "I have to go. I'll be in touch with you. You did for me what I asked you to. That man got what he deserved." Beckman gathered up his coat and started for the door. "Thank you. I'll be in touch," he repeated. Then he was gone.

"Wow," I muttered, "you wouldn't think that little nothing of a turtle-crazed loon could get so angry, killing the young girl, even smashing up the little turtles he'd given her. A total maniac."

"Still waters run deep," Susan muttered.

"And muddy," I added. "Henny, how are you? Your evening must have been a torture."

"I don't want to talk about it." He glanced at me and shrugged. "I'll see you in the office on Monday." He found his coat and left.

"Henny really fell for Daria," I said. "I'll bet he thought she might be the one. I really feel sorry for him."

"He's still in a fall, but not for Daria," Susan said.

"What do you mean?"

"He's crushed by more than Daria. I'll bet he's wondering why the universe has it in for him."

"I don't doubt it. Maybe we'll get an interesting case that'll get his mind back in the proper track."

Susan rose. "I'm going to take a nap, then write up this story. I'd like to get it into Monday's paper." She headed for my bedroom but paused, smiled, and said, "Don't bother me."

I didn't, but that night we ate in Giandos and spent a lazy Sunday together. Not once all day did Susan complain about my bothering her.

Eleven

Henny already sat at his desk, a display of toothpicks spread out before him, when I arrived in the office Monday morning. He didn't look up as I entered and went to the coffee machine.

I took a breath and asked, "How are you? Coffee?"

"Worst crime family *ever*," he answered, rapping his knuckles on his desk. The nearest toothpicks jumped. He expressed no interest in coffee.

Momentarily speechless, I simply gazed Henny's way. Finally, he looked at me. "They had to be the dumbest, clumsiest criminals since... since... since Professor Moriarty allowed himself to be shoved over the falls by Sherlock."

"I didn't know you read that far back in the history of crime."

"You underestimate me."

I cleared my throat. "Yeah, hard to figure what was going through their heads."

"And *both* of them! Must have been something genetic."

"It could always have been worse," I said, taking my chair, coffee cup in hand.

"Worse? How?"

"She could have roped you in. Seemed to be heading in that direction. You could have slid into something... permanent, almost permanent... with a murderess."

Henny moaned. "I really liked her. I didn't tell you. She wanted me to do something."

"Do something? What do you mean?"

"I mean something to get her off the hook. I was a smart detective, she said. Couldn't I think of a way out... to get her off?"

"She admitted to killing her uncle? When was this?"

"Over dinner at Giandos. I'd danced around the topic and dropped enough hints that she finally concluded *we*, me and you, had figured out what happened between her and her uncle. The look on her face when she saw Thursday and the two guys with him coming over to the table..." Henny shook his head sadly. "She started in on how it was an accident. Her uncle attacked her. She didn't mean it. It just happened... and all at the top of her lungs and in tears. I wanted to drape a napkin over my face. I hope they let me back into Giandos."

"You think she specifically went to his place to... to kill him?"

Henny shrugged. "It doesn't much matter to Uncle Randall, and it doesn't matter to me. Now." He paused for a moment. "No, I think something happened and things got out of hand. She grabbed something and bashed his head in."

"You should consider it a lucky escape," I offered.

"Yeah, yeah. I know." He glanced over at me. "Doesn't help."

"No, I guess not." We sat quietly for a few moments. Then I asked, "What happens to all of their money?"

"Who cares. I hope the turtles get it."

"They're going to the Bronx Zoo. Says Susan."

The fate of the turtles ended the conversation until, some thirty minutes later, Paul Beckman arrived in the office. He professed his gratitude for the help we'd provided and left us a check for five thousand dollars, wishing he could make it more. That made two of us, but, under the circumstances, I couldn't complain. He left, heading back to Jersey City.

The morning proceeded quietly until the office phone rang. I picked up and welcomed the request by a lawyer named Reginald Towers for a one o'clock appointment. He said it involved investigating an inheritance claim, and he'd explain more fully when we were together.

"A new case. It'll take your mind off your troubles," I counseled Henny.

He snorted and we idled away the day until one.

Reginald Towers proved to be an older, white-haired, white-mustached gentleman. He wore a gray pinstriped suit beneath his tan camel-hair overcoat. Henny ushered him into our client chair, today positioned before Henny's desk. I could sense he'd impressed Henny, especially the pinstriped part.

"I'm Henny. This is Lloyd." Henny positioned his desk chair as if its exact orientation mattered. He seemed to have, temporarily at least, surfaced from the murky depths of Daria Givens. "How can we help you?

"I've noticed certain mentions of you in the newspapers, mostly the *Post*."

'Thank you, Susan' ran through my brain.

"I have a situation which would otherwise play itself out in the courts, but in this instance needs the talents you gentlemen seem to possess."

I thought Mr. Towers might prove to be a very compatible client.

"As I said on the phone, it's an inheritance case. A great deal of money is on the line, and I am... leery, to put it mildly... about the heir apparent."

"Tell us about it," Henny urged, popping a clean toothpick into the corner of his mouth.

"I was the legal representative for Warren Goldman for nearly forty years. We became good friends over that span. He passed away three months ago, and his estate of ten million dollars is at stake. You will, I hope, forgive me if I appear to be long-winded, but I must give you the background."

Henny asked, "Did Mr. Goldman leave a will?"

"I'll get to that in time."

"Sorry," Henny muttered. "Tell your tale."

"Warren had—and I advisedly use the past tense—had a daughter. His wife died young, and he had the means to raise his daughter in some luxury. He made his money in the stock market. For some inexplicable reason, though, the parenting didn't go well. Jessica was eight when she lost her mother. Warren never remarried. This was some thirty years ago. When Jessica became a teenager, she grew hostile. I really can't say what set her off. Warren and I discussed it over more bottles of scotch than you can count, but we never arrived at any sensible conclusion. From age thirteen to seventeen, Jessica fought her father at every turn. Her school attendance dropped off. And at Stuyvesant High School! I'm sure you know about Stuyvesant."

Stuyvesant was the premier academic high school in New York City. Its acceptance rate was very low—there was an entrance test—and, being part of the New York school system, it was free.

"Her Stuyvesant friends, the ones we met, were, shall I say, a little dicey, the way they dressed, how they smoked, God knows what else. And at that age."

Towers paused and I offered him coffee or some water. He seemed a bit too upper crust to be offered a taste of *Boone's That's All*. He did accept the bottle of water, though, but asked for a glass to drink it from. I accommodated him with a cardboard coffee cup.

"Before Jessica turned eighteen, she ran away. Just up and left, along with some of her Stuyvesant friends. Warren spent a boatload of money trying to find her. He found out approximately where she was, somewhere in Maine, but he never managed to pinpoint her, much less bring her home. Let me assure you, he never stopped trying to find her, never stopped loving her, never stopped hoping for that one magical phone call or knock on the door. But it didn't happen. Then we got word that she was dead. An unexplained accident in the Maine woods. By the time the Maine authorities in Cotters Grove, the nearest town, had investigated and learned her antecedents and sent the news to Warren, she'd already been buried. He never saw her again after she left home at seventeen. Didn't even get a chance for a final farewell."

"How long ago did you say her death occurred?" I asked.

"Jessica would have been twenty when we received word of her passing. And that would be some eighteen years ago, the summer of 2006. Warren had nothing after that but his work. For those previous three years, though, he'd searched for her, hoped for her, constantly. He wasn't a religious man, but I know he prayed for her to return. But..." Towers shrugged and looked down for a moment. "You mentioned his will. He never changed his will. Well, that's not strictly true. Whatever slim ration of hope he lived on, hoping for Jessica's return, was the belief that the report of her death was in error. Since he'd never seen her since she originally left, the door for a miracle remained open, if only a crack. In his will she was his sole, number one beneficiary. If, however, she truly was dead, he left a list of others who would share in the inheritance. I should tell you he was cremated, according to his wishes."

Towers stopped talking. I felt a vague premonition about what was coming next, and asked, "And what is the problem now with the inheritance?"

"Jessica has come back to claim it."

"The dead daughter?" Henny sputtered.

"Yes and no," Towers answered. "She says she is Jessica Goldman. But I don't believe her."

"You don't recognize her?" I asked. "You knew her, right?"

"I did know her. I'd seen her now and then when I did work for Warren, and no, I don't recognize her. When she left at seventeen, she was thin and whole. By whole I mean no nose rings, no long line of earring studs up and down both ears, no tattoos."

"And now she has all of these?" Henny asked.

"She does."

"She's about thirty-eight, you said?" I asked.

"Yes."

"And has all of those add-ons?" Henny asked again.

"Yes. She answered some basic questions you might think only Jessica would know, but Jessica could have told this person about her past before she died. Or this woman could have been someone who ran away with her and knew her back when she lived with Warren. Or I could have been asking the wrong questions. I don't know, but I simply don't think this woman who showed up on our doorstep after Warren's death is his daughter. I mean how could she be? The Maine authorities couldn't be so incompetent as to muck up something like that."

"And you'd like Henny and me to do an investigation."

"Exactly."

"Do you think she'll talk to us?" Henny asked.

"For ten million dollars, I'm sure she'll talk to the man in the moon if she has to."

"What would you prefer?" I asked. "Not that it will influence us one way or the other. Do you hope it's Jessica or do you hope it's not?"

"I prefer that the last thing to ever happen to Warren in his life and after-life not be his getting scammed out of his life's work."

Towers tone had taken on an edge.

"Do you have an amicable relationship with the woman who showed up?" Henny asked.

"I wouldn't call it so. Professional relationship, maybe. She's quite aware I have my doubts about her... authenticity. But I can contact her. Is that what you're asking? I'm allowing her to stay in her father's apartment. Her old apartment, according to her."

"Yes. Tell her to expect to hear from the Henny and Lloyd Agency."

"I can give you her contact information right now, and I'll send you a text or call you after I alert her to expect to hear from you."

"That'll work," I said. We exchanged information and after a brief discussion, Mr. Towers wrote out a check for ten thousand dollars and gave us an assurance that any expenses we might incur would be met. I'd been right. Reginald Towers had proven to be a very compatible client.

Twelve

We didn't have to wait for Reginald Towers to call and give us the go-ahead to contact Jessica Goldman. The woman called us herself, proclaiming her eagerness to cooperate with anyone whose goal was to prove she was who she said she was. She promised she would be in our office at four o'clock.

"She sounds awfully sure of herself," Henny commented.

"Yeah. Bold and ballsy or dead certain?"

"Funny you should mention dead."

"Isn't it, though. Somebody became dead eighteen years ago, it seems."

"Somebody the cops in Maine determined was Jessica Goldman."

"What would Sam Spade do?" I asked.

"He'd go to Maine and poke around. Even been to Maine?"

"No. In fact, I don't recall ever even saying 'Maine' in my daily life until today."

"Cotters Grove. I wonder if it's even still there," Henny posed.

"Let's find out." I revved up our official office HP laptop and found that Cotters Grove did exist and boasted seven thousand inhabitants, up from only fifteen hundred in the 2000 census.

"And Jessica ran away in, what, 2003?" I added.

Henny scribbled some numbers on a pad in front of him. "Looks like. She's thirty-eight now, so born in 1986; age seventeen in 2003."

I returned to the laptop and read, "Cotters Grove is located in the western part of the state near the Canadian and New Hampshire borders, and its claim to fame is supplying its fair share of Christmas trees to the world... or at least to the East Coast and Canada."

"Hmmm," Henny groused. "Cotters Grove 2003 makes Coblesburg look like a major metropolis." A recent case had sent Henny and me to a small town in upstate New York. Two nights there had made us long for the noise and aggravation of New York City. But the case had ended successfully, so no complaints.

"Flip you a coin for who goes to Chinatown and brings back lunch," I suggested. "We got about three hours to kill."

"No need. I'll go." Henny'd held up well so far after his miserable weekend, and I wasn't about to argue with him.

When he returned with some General Tso's chicken and two orders of scallion pancakes, we reheated everything and had a leisurely meal and an idle afternoon. At three-fifty, we heard the grinding and wheezing of our elevator. A few minutes later, in walked—without knocking—the woman purporting to be Jessica Goldman.

Henny dealt with her coat while I looked her over. She was larger than I'd imagined. I had a slim, seventeen-year-old teenager bouncing around in my mind. I tossed that image away quickly. This Jessica stood maybe five-eight and was built sturdily, not fat, simply big. A line of silver pellets lined each ear, and a small, black something hung from her nose. It looked like she'd snuffed up a spider but hadn't managed to get the last couple legs into her nostrils. Her hair was long and sandy brown, tied back in a ponytail. Tattoos poked out of her sleeves and the neck of her red T-shirt. I indicated our client chair, and she sat and marked her territory immediately.

"I'm Jessica Goldman."

I laid the problem on the table. "I'm Lloyd. He's Henny. I understand there's a concern over your identity."

"I don't know why there should be. I freakin' know who I am."

"That's likely true," I agreed, "but you can understand how, under the circumstances, and with so much money involved, the responsible people want to be certain about things."

"Great. Be responsible. I can answer any question anybody wants to ask me. I can name my kindergarten teacher. I can do DNA. Why don't they do DNA?"

I answered, "Mr. Towers says your father was cremated. Maybe there is no DNA."

Henny asked, "Do you have any family members they could compare your DNA with?"

Jessica's face drew blank. "Family members? I don't know. My mother was an only child, and she's gone. My father's of no help, but there's gotta be a way. Shouldn't they have to prove I'm *not* who I say I am?"

"They say it's difficult to prove a negative," Henny said.

Jessica moaned. "Everybody's got an excuse."

"How about you tell us your story," I suggested.

"Are you two here to help me or hurt me?" she asked.

"Neither," Henny assured her. "We've been hired to find the truth of the matter. We don't care who gets your father's millions, only that they go to the right place."

"The right place? Like that list of ten cockadoodles he's lined up to dish out a million bucks each to? That's the right place? I hope you're starting to get a picture of why I couldn't live with him any longer than I did. He was always doing crap like that, holding things over my head. 'Look what you'll be getting one day.' 'Imagine how lucky you are.' 'Don't bring people like that home with you. They're only interested in using you.' I could go on. Want me to?"

"No, no need," I said. "Where did you run away to, and who did you run away with? How did you live then? How have you managed these past twenty-one years?"

Jessica heaved a mighty sigh, then talked for some forty-five minutes.

She and four high school pals, two male and two female, decided that their grievances against the older generation were so profound that nothing would suit but to run off and start new lives. Each gathered what money they could, Jessica providing the bulk of it, and this mini-migration headed north toward the border. They floated back and forth for a month or two between Maine and Canada before settling in near tiny Cotters Grove along with another group of a half-dozen teenagers they had come across with similar grievances against their elders. They took up residence in a deserted logging camp, where some half-a-dozen cabins remained habitable, complete with bunkbeds.

Jessica's father dogged her tracks, though. Her friends learned to sniff out the occasional stranger who showed up asking questions about a missing girl. Gradually, the group she lived with broke up, most of them afraid they'd be located by their parents because of the attention Jessica attracted. Jessica became a *persona non grata* and after three years was forced to go out on her own, there being only herself and one other young woman left in camp.

Henny scratched his head. "Can you explain how the Cotters Grove police came up with a dead body and finally determined it was you?"

"Sure. Statute of limitations is long up for anything," she said with a giggle.

It struck me that Jessica had grown and matured as nature demanded in the past twenty-one years, but her mindset and reactions and thought processes had remained distinctly teenage.

"As you see, it wasn't me they found. It was a girl we knew only as Sparkle." Jessica shrugged. "It was that kind of a time. Sparkle was a lousy thief. I don't mean she had no skill at stealing. I mean she was a louse because she stole. She stayed in camp as long as she did because there was always stuff she could steal from others and finally from me. One day she went off and didn't return. I expected her to come back to the cabin with... with some supplies or money. We were supposed to be helping each other out, you know? But she never did return, and I wasn't about to live in the woods alone, so I cleaned myself up the best I could, but when I went looking for my wallet—which, by the way, I took great pains to hide—and whatever else that was worth taking with me, I couldn't find a thing. I was officially a nobody. That little bitch stole whatever she could lay her hands on, my identity last of all. I'm as sure of it now as I was then. I was always afraid my father would send the right person who could find me, and I didn't want that. He didn't let up, my father. When I heard they'd found *my* body in the woods... I knew it was Sparkle; it had to be, but I didn't care. I figured they found the stuff she stole from me in her pockets, my wallet, especially. Then it struck me! If my father thought I was dead, he'd stop looking for me, and that would suit me fine. When I heard they thought it was me they found, no way did I correct the cops. I let them think it was me. So what?

"You know, I've always wondered what shape Sparkle was in when they found her. There are animals in the woods." Jessica shrugged. "Hungry animals, maybe? I don't know and didn't care. But it appeared from the little I read in the weekly newspaper and the bits of gossip I picked up in town that the cops depended on the identification they found on her. My identification. Maybe she had none of her own. Didn't care then; don't care now. Weeks and then a month went by, and the excitement died away.

"I managed to find work in Cotters Grove for a while. People in town only knew me as one of the kids from the logging camp... if they knew me at all. We didn't hang around in town much. Anyway, I used a phony name and found work, eventually got bored and moved along.

"My moving along story isn't relevant. Eighteen years passed with no pressure from my father. I felt free. I lived my life. When I found out on a library computer that my father had died, I relented and decided to allow the old man to take care of me for the rest of my life—as long as he wasn't really there to take care of me." She flapped her hands open in the manner of a playful seal. "Here I am; I'm alive; and I want my inheritance. That's the story. So, can you two sharpsters get me to the other side of this to where the money is? If you do, I'll pay you." She got to her feet.

Henny and I rose, too. I hadn't found Jessica to be a very appealing personage, so I let Henny respond to her.

"We'll do our best, Ms. Goldman," he promised. "As long as you're not afraid of the truth, then..." He mimicked her flap of the hands. "...you have nothing to be afraid of."

I thought Jessica might take offense at Henny's flippancy, but she simply laughed. "Anything you need, give me a call. I'm staying at my father's place for now. Mr. Towers gave me a cell phone. Here's the number. And, please, no Ms. Goldman. I'm Jessica."

Henny retrieved her coat and helped her on with it. When she departed, Henny and I returned to our desks and discussed the case over a short *Boone's That's All,* but the *Boone's* proved much more entertaining than Jessica Goldman's problem.

Later, after dinner at home, I called Susan, who, naturally, had a decent idea or two. I'd begun to get over my resentment at her always coming up with more ideas regarding our cases than Henny and I did. I hated to think she had superior investigatory skills to us, but that's often how it seemed. Of late, though I had gravitated to the belief that Henny and I could hold our own against her. I knew, though, that we were better with her than without her, and I was certainly happier with her than without her.

Thirteen

The next morning in the office I said to Henny, "Susan had a good suggestion last night when I talked to her."

"I was afraid you wouldn't call her."

"Why wouldn't I call her?" I asked in a huff.

"That's why."

"What's why?"

"Your snooty attitude about our depending on her so much."

"We don't depend on her 'so much'." She helps out when she can."

Henny chuckled. "When can't she?"

"What's funny?"

"You are."

I took a calming breath. "Do you want to hear what she said or not?"

"Of course I do. Fire away."

I didn't like Henny's pointing out my display of an attitude I thought I'd brought under control, if not entirely overcome, but I let the moment slide.

"Ask Jessica for the names of the high school dropouts she ran away with, then track them down. They might be able to confirm that it wasn't Jessica but really Sparkle whose body was found in the woods. Some of them might even be willing and able to identify Jessica as she looks now."

"She's changed a lot physically since then," Henny pointed out.

"Bah! Their talking together would confirm their identities to one another. Do you think if they put a wall between you and me, I couldn't convince you I was Lloyd, and you couldn't convince me you were Henny if we spoke?"

Henny nodded thoughtfully. "I see what you mean. Good point."

"Susan thought if we could get a yearbook from Jessica's time in Stuyvesant, we might uncover other friendships, other ways to confirm or deny Jessica's identity. And Susan pointed out we didn't ask whether Sparkle was one of the Stuyvesant gang or someone Jessica met at the camp."

"If they only knew her as Sparkle, she must have been from somewhere else, otherwise they certainly would have known her name."

"Maybe. Maybe she was known as Sparkle in Stuyvesant."

Henny frowned. "Could be, but I doubt it. He rose from his desk and walked to the windows. "It's a reasonably nice day out. I'll make the walk to Stuyvesant. They must keep yearbooks on record. While I'm gone, why don't you book us a car and plot out a trip to Cotters Grove?"

"You really think we need to go all the way to freakin' Maine?" I asked, thinking of the temperature drop in my future if the trip came off.

"Sure. At least one of us does. If we can prove it *wasn't* Jessica's body in the woods..." He snapped the fingers on his right hand. "...there you go. It would mean she's likely still alive and ten million dollars richer."

"I guess so. I hope Jessica likes to tip."

"She said she'd pay," Henny added as he suited up for his winter walk, and I got to trip-planning. The only thing involved in planning a trip to Maine was renting a car. I'd done that recently for our jaunt to Coblesburg, so I had experience. After I reserved the car, I took the initiative and called Jessica, who assured me Sparkle was not a New York City girl. Ohio, she thought, but wasn't sure. She repeated to me that no one ever knew Sparkle's given name and effectively closed off that avenue for me. She claimed to remember only two of the names from Stuyvesant who ran off with her. The ones she'd forgotten, she assured me, weren't friends of hers, but simply joined in and kept to themselves the time they spent in the camp. She recalled them going off on their own a few months after arriving, as soon as the cold weather set in. The names she did remember were David Benevides and Priscilla Moy, and she assured me she had no idea where they'd gotten to. She also preferred they continue to know nothing about her except that she was dead.

"They may still think it's share and share alike," she said, giggling. "It's not."

When I told her Henny and I were planning a trip to Cotters Grove, she laughed again.

"More power to you. Perfect time of year for it. Good luck if you get any temperatures above zero, but the sooner you verify me, the better. I wish you success."

Henny arrived back in the office a couple hours later with a yearbook under his arm and two orders of moo shu pork. As we folded our pancakes and nibbled, we brought each other up to date.

"All she could give you was two names?" Henny asked.

"That's it. And she knows nothing about their whereabouts. How'd you get the yearbook?"

"Slipped it under my jacket from the school library. Jessica never graduated, so the best I could get was her junior yearbook. I checked and she's in it. Maybe we can find those other two names."

"For whatever good it'll do."

"Maybe it'll be like one of those diagrams with circles looping in with one another."

I thought for a moment. "A Venn diagram?"

Henny grabbed a pen and a piece of paper and drew circles.

"Yeah," I said, "that's a Venn diagram."

"Whatever. This person might know that person who might know this person who might know what happened to David Benevides or Priscilla Moy."

I shrugged. "We'll see."

Henny's detective instincts, always sharp, proved dead on, though.

Priscilla Moy showed up in four photos next to a fellow named Rafael Wallingford. A quick trip through Facebook found a Rafael Wallingford living in New York City, married with two children, who worked in publishing.

"What did I tell you?" Henny gloated.

"Good call..."

Henny stopped me. "I'll make the trip to Maine. You don't really want to go, do you?"

"No, I don't. You do?"

Henny shrugged. "New York is a bit burdensome to me at present. I'd rather be out and about. And one of us should be here in the city looking into this."

"The car's rented for tomorrow. You know where we picked up the other one. Same place. I'll go with you to get it."

"You track down everything you can here."

"Starting with Rafael Wallingford."

"Yes. Finish your last pancake and send him a Facebook message. And don't forget the other two names. I'll try to figure out what I expect to research in Cotters Grove."

We cleaned up after lunch and set to work. Before we got much done, though, Reginald Towers stopped in. We offered him the client chair and coffee.

"So, what have you found out?" he asked.

"Mr. Towers," Henny responded. I could tell from Henny's tone, something good was on its way. "May I ask you a question?"

"Of course."

"You might find it offensive. I don't mean it that way, but Lloyd and I are in the business of asking questions, and who knows what piece of information will turn out to be helpful?"

"Good lord. Just ask."

"The list of people who will receive bequests if Jessica isn't Jessica. Are you on that list?"

Towers flinched, but only a little.

"Yes, yes I am. I was Warren Goldman's lawyer and friend for a very long time. I told you that."

Henny held up his hand as a stop sign. "Please... I'm not asking you to justify Mr. Goldman's desires. He was free to do whatever he wanted with his money."

Towers gave a small *harrumph* and settled back in his chair.

"You said ten people were on the list and ten million dollars... would that be a million each or is it divided some other way."

"A million each... or more precisely ten percent of his worldly goods to each of the ten."

"I see," Henny said softly.

"Now, back to my question," Towers said. "Have you determined anything?"

I answered. "We've gotten a couple of names we can research. Henny is driving to Maine tomorrow to visit Cotters Grove. You'll probably be gone for the rest of the week, don't you think?"

"Most likely," Henny agreed.

"What do you expect to find up there?"

"Well, we thought if we could somehow prove that the young woman they identified as Jessica was *not* Jessica, it would go a long way to proving that Jessica was still alive. Plus, the people Lloyd hopes to get in touch with might very well be able to identify Jessica, since they were together for a while back during the time in question."

"Yes, good, good. I'm glad to see you're taking an aggressive approach. I approve."

Neither Henny nor I thanked him for his approval other than by silent acquiescence.

Henny asked. "And there's no way we can do anything in the way of DNA testing?"

"I told you. The man was cremated."

"So you did," Henny answered. "Family members? Aunts, uncles?"

"None." Towers got to his feet. "Good luck on your trip." To me, he said, "Keep me up to date as soon as you know anything definitive. We can't let this linger on."

We bid one another farewell. Henny went home to prepare for his trip the next day, and I set out to find a way to reach Rafael Wallingford.

Fourteen

The next morning, I accompanied Henny to the car rental office on Tenth Avenue and saw him off, telling him to stay warm. He grunted me a farewell and headed to the West Side Highway and parts north. I took a cab to Centre Street and welcomed the stultifying heat of our office. I welcomed it so much that I cracked open a window to keep myself from swooning. Henny would have enjoyed my use of "swooning," a totally forties' word. Think Frank Sinatra if you're able to. I'd picked up quite a bit about the forties from Henny.

At any rate, I went to our computer to check on whether Rafael Wallingford had responded to the Facebook message I'd sent him the day before. I assumed that most of everything flying around on Facebook got ignored, so it knocked me back a few steps when I saw he'd responded.

In my message to him, I said I was trying to locate some classmates from Stuyvesant High School from the early 2000s.

This wasn't a lie. *They* were classmates, but I never claimed they were *my* classmates. Rafael seemed eager to talk about the past. The greatest years of our life, he claimed; no responsibilities other than getting your paper in when it was due; the only time in our lives we'd be surrounded by certifiably intelligent people. He'd like to meet and catch up.

It surprised me he didn't ask more about me, but no looking a gift horse, etc. He worked on Thirty-Fourth Street and where would I like to meet? I suggested Bocca di Bacco at seven o'clock. I could get there early for some of their mushroom bruschetta and then see what Rafael had to offer. I sent the message back to him and before long, he said yes, he'd be looking forward to it.

~ * ~

The bartender had just taken away my plate when Rafael entered the restaurant. He was easy to spot. The dark, thick mustache he sported matched his latest photos on Facebook. He ran his eye over the sparse crowd in the restaurant, including running his eye over me. Since I would have been about ready for first grade during his junior year, the time in question, he knew at a glance I'd never been a classmate of his. My stomach did a little jump, hoping Rafael didn't get upset about my dragging him fourteen blocks downtown under sort of false pretenses. I rose from my bar chair and beckoned him.

He tilted his head quizzically and walked my way.

"Rafael Wallingford?" I asked, giving him my most engaging smile.

"Are you Lloyd? From Facebook?"

"Yes, yes, I am." I gestured to the bar. "Please, belly up." I hoped he was the bellying up kind of guy. "Order a drink and let me explain."

The bar was backed by a mirror and rows of bottles, all backlit by red light shining from below. The red light introduced an aura of creepiness into the moment as Rafael sat and I gestured for the bartender. He ordered a Kendall Jackson chardonnay, and my merlot, half gone by now, sat at the ready.

"What's this all about?" he asked. "Who are you? You can't have been in my class."

It struck me that if he'd really been concerned about the situation, he would have waited until after my explanation before he ordered his wine. Since he'd ordered the wine, though, he obviously planned to listen to what I had to say for at least as long as his glass of wine held out. First, I explained who I was.

"Private eye, wow!" He lifted his glass and tilted it toward me in a toast. "You must lead an interesting life."

"There are occasional bursts of excitement," I agreed. I didn't clue Rafael in on the hours I spent in the office reading the 1940s' mysteries Henny passed on to me, or the time Henny spent fussing with toothpicks spread out across his desk. "We've been hired for a case that involves some people you may well have once known."

"Oh, the classmate angle."

"Exactly. Your junior year." I smiled, I hoped, charmingly. "Remember back that far?"

"Who are we talking about?"

"Do you recall a group of your classmates having dropped out of school and disappearing toward the end of their and your junior year? I have a few names." I gave him the three names I had. David Benevides, Cynthia Moy, and of course, Jessica Goldman.

Rafael shifted into pensive mode and sipped his wine. "Disappearing, yes. I do remember. Two names don't ring a bell, but yes, Cynthia Moy and I were on the debating team that year. She stopped participating, I recall, in the second semester. Their dropping out was a hot topic for a while."

"Can you recall any other names? I mean of those who left the school then."

"No, no," he said slowly. "But I had a girlfriend, sort of a girlfriend, back then. Gina Planter. She talked a lot about it. I think she knew one of the girls who took off."

"Jessica or Cynthia?"

Rafael slowly shook his head. "No, no. She might have mentioned them, but neither one of them was the one she was friendly with. The name will come to me."

"Is Gina still around?" I asked. "Can I talk to her?" For a moment I thought I had something, but Rafael quashed my hope.

"Gina. Oh, boy. I don't know where she is."

But then he reignited it.

"Maybe Lourdes Gonzalez would know. Lourdes was always Miss Social. Then and now. Voted prom queen senior year. She still organizes reunions, sends out newsletters, and generally keeps in touch with the people who graduated with her. If anyone knows what happened to Gina, or the people you mentioned, she would. What's this all about, anyway?"

I explained Jessica Goldman's situation.

"Jessica Goldman, no, I cannot place her. There were hundreds of kids in the junior class." He shook his head. "I got nothing. And ten million dollars. My goodness. My parents always told me that graduating from Stuyvesant would assure a student's future." He laughed.

"Not exactly what they meant, though, eh?"

We chatted a bit more about the ins and outs of the case. Rafael was especially interested in how it turned out that Jessica was thought dead, then turned up alive. We agreed it was the core of the case.

When Rafael put his empty wineglass back on the bar, he got off his chair and said, "Do you have a card or something? I'll get in touch with Lourdes and mention... maybe you better write those names down for me. Here's my number. Text me the names."

I texted him the three names, and he checked to be sure he received the information.

"Let me know how it turns out," he said, reaching out to shake hands.

"I will," I promised. "If it turns out you've been a crucial help, maybe Jessica will throw a million your way."

"Ha! That'll be the day. Nice talking to you."

Rafael left wearing a smile, and I ordered another merlot, favorably impressed by this particular Stuyvesant grad.

~ * ~

Henny gave me a call that night from somewhere in New Hampshire to assure me he'd had a nice dinner, and he'd be in Cotters Grove early tomorrow, depending on what time he woke up next morning. I wished him well and gave him a recounting of my visit with Rafael Wallingford. He complimented me on making progress and told me to keep him up to date, something I would have done without his prompting.

~ * ~

I could hear the office phone ringing when I stepped off the elevator next morning and hustled down the hallway, digging in my pocket for the office door key. I managed to reach the phone in time.

"Henny and Lloyd Agency."

"This is Reginald Towers. I called to ask if you'd made any progress."

"In fact, I have." I filled him in on my visit with Rafael.

"Keep at it. Jessica, if she is Jessica, is demanding we settle the estate. I could be disbarred if I'm caught screwing around and intentionally delaying things. Once I hand over the money to her, it will be a nightmare trying to get it back. I mean if we find out too late she's not Jessica."

"I understand. Henny's working on things in Maine, and I have people to contact who may prove the truth one way or the other about Jessica."

Towers encouraged me to be thorough and quick, and we hung up. No sooner had I replaced the phone than it rang again. I wondered what Towers had forgotten to tell me, but no, Jessica was on the line this time.

"Have you managed yet to prove I'm me?" she asked. "I think Mr. Towers is jerking me around. You should hear the legal bull he tosses my way. If he doesn't come across soon, I'm going to escalate this whole thing. I can get my own lawyer, you know. I'll sue him."

"I'm sure you can."

"Look, let me hire you to prove my identity. You seem pretty sharp."

"Thank you, but Mr. Towers has already hired Henny and me for pretty much the same reason. You both want an answer to the same question, so... That's what we're trying to find."

We sparred a bit more, but she finally understood the ethics of Henny and me not serving two masters. She ended by say, "I'd thought I'd be welcomed back after all these years when people heard my explanation, but this... It's Mr. Towers trying to block me and get a million bucks for himself. I know you'll help me."

For the umpteenth time, I assured her that Henny and I were after the truth, so she had nothing to worry about, and we said goodbye.

I popped a pod into our coffee machine and made myself a cup, but as soon I'd taken my first sip, the office phone rang again. I wondered why things were never this busy when Henny was here. This time it was Rafael Wallingford. We exchanged good mornings, and Rafael said he had some information.

"I had a phone conversation with Lourdes last night. She's very excited. Anything that's newsworthy about our graduating class gets her heart pumping." He gave a short laugh. "She remembered the disappearance of the five runaways and recalled the guidance department interviewing students to see what they knew about the incident. You can add two names to the ones you have. Shelley Mak and Timothy Brown. Now, there's good news and bad. Which would you like first?"

I did not appreciate Rafael's playful mood, but I wasn't about to alienate him.

"Hit me with the bad news so I'll still have something to look forward to."

Rafael gave another little laugh, which I didn't share.

"Okay, Timothy Brown has passed away. Three years ago, so I don't suppose he'll be of any help."

"And the good news?"

"Lourdes is still in touch with Shelley Mak, or at least she was six months ago when she sent out the most recent newsletter. Lourdes can't wait for the resolution of this current situation. She figures she'll have the best newsletter ever to send out."

"And Shelley Mak?" I urged.

"Lives in Staten Island. I can give you her contact information."

"Text it to me. What about your old girlfriend?" I asked.

"Lourdes tells me she moved to France. When she told me that, I remembered what a whiz Gina was in French class, so it didn't surprise me."

"Does she have contact information for Gina?"

"Home address and email address."

"What about David Benevides and Priscilla Moy?"

"Nothing in her files. When they ran away, they must have kept running. They've evaporated."

"Okay, thanks. You've given me something to work with. Oh, did you ask Lourdes whether she had any strong memory of Jessica Goldman?"

"I did. Lourdes got out a yearbook and found a picture of her, but it didn't ring any bells."

"I see. Thanks again. I know you'll want to hear how things turn out..."

"Right, and Lourdes needs to know for her newsletter."

"Right, her newsletter. I'll keep you in the loop."

"That'd be great."

We said goodbye and a few minutes later, my phone made its notification noise. Rafael had sent me Shelley Mak's information, and I foresaw a trip to Staten Island in my future.

Fifteen

I hadn't been to Staten Island in forever, and to tell the truth, I wanted to get the visit over with as soon as possible. So, I emailed Shelley Mak and made my case. Thankfully, she replied almost right away with her cell number, and I made the call, soon giving belated thanks to the COVID pandemic because Ms. Mak currently worked from home for American Express. I went a little deeper, explaining to her about the legal need to identify Jessica Goldman.

"Oh lord. I never thought such a preposterous period of my life would ever come up again," was her reaction. "How did you find me?"

I told her about Lourdes and got a chuckle in return.

"I should have guessed. I'm on her mailing list. Her newsletters are usually interesting. I'm really sorry I never graduated from Stuy, but what's done is done. I thought Jessica Goldman was dead. That's what I read in a list of the recently deceased in one of Lourdes' back newsletters. It turns out I'd left the compound—logging camp, really—and was roaming around the country when it happened—considerably further south, if you follow me. But when I finally returned to New York, my parents took me back and gave me time to get myself together, which I did. I returned to New York City about a year, year-and-a-half after she supposedly died. That's when I found out about her."

"So, four or five years after the group of you took off."

"I'd say so."

"Do you think we can meet and talk about this?"

"Sure, why not. You'll have to come to Staten Island, though. I'm not traipsing into the city."

"Not a problem. Is this still your address?" I read from what Rafael gave me.

"Sure. Want to come now? I have to be on a conference call at five o'clock. Plenty of time to chat if you leave now."

"Then I'll leave now."

After texting Henny about my uncovering one of Jessica's runaway companions and my imminent meeting with her, I took advantage of Mr. Towers kind offer of unlimited expenses and took a cab to Staten Island, making certain to get a receipt.

Shelley Mak lived in a townhouse community named Pleasant Shores, and from the short drive through it to her address, it appeared to live up to its name. Not pleasant enough, however, to get me to abandon the city and relocate there in this lifetime, but to each his or her own. Shelley welcomed me at the door, wearing a lime green pants suit and low-heeled black shoes. I immediately noticed a photo on an end table of her, a man, and a young boy.

After we exchanged greetings, I indicated the photo. "Your family?"

"Yes. Bill is my husband and Billy junior my son. He's eleven."

"Attractive gentlemen," I said, hoping to be ingratiating.

"I like them," she answered with a smile.

We sat and I declined any refreshment.

"What do you want to know?" Shelley asked. She still looked in good shape.

"As I mentioned, we're trying to determine whether the woman who showed up claiming to be Jessica Goldman really is Jessica Goldman. Ten million dollars is at stake."

Shelley's eyes widened. "How so?"

"An inheritance from her father."

Shelley gave me a puzzled look. "Can't they do a DNA test?"

I offered a friendly grin. "Jessica has DNA, but her father's went up in smoke. Cremated."

"No cousins, aunts, uncles?"

"Not that she knows of.

"So, her father died. Boy, I recall him."

"You met him?"

"No, I didn't meet him, but he appeared to go off the deep end when Jessy ran off."

"How friendly were you with Jessica?"

"Friendly enough to take her seriously when I heard she and the others planned to run away to Maine. I wasn't all that happy living at home, myself. School was a mountain load of work, which, back then, I didn't see the need for. I went to Stuy because my parents made me take the test and, lucky me, I passed. Premier high school in New York at no cost. No way I could wiggle out of that."

"I see your point. So, you joined the escapees."

"I did. We took a bus... Jessica, I recall, paid for the tickets. I can't imagine what I thought I was going to do when I got to Maine." She gave a forlorn chuckle. "If we knew then what we know now, eh?" She shrugged. "Things went way off the track before too long. Very little money. I never imagined I'd have to work—none of us did, I guess. But we picked up little jobs here and there, same as the bunch of kids we joined at the camp. Do you know about the logging camp?"

"Yeah, it's where you stayed."

"It's where we argued and fought."

"Why fought?"

She laughed. "We thought we were running away to Eden. No. Try living on your own in the freezing cold woods with no money and nothing really to do, along with a bunch of other kids you didn't even know. And finally, being hounded by Jessy's father, who sent, my god, detectives, snoops, investigators, who knows how many people to find his daughter. He must have spent a bundle looking for her. We spent half our time hiding Jessy and lying to people asking about her. She was always afraid her father would walk into camp one day. It really ticked off the other bunch of kids, who came from all over. They did not want any news of where they were getting out, and I was afraid they'd turn Jessy in just to get rid of her. Naturally, if Jessy got caught, the four of us from Stuy with her would be in jeopardy. One girl especially, from the other group, wanted no parts of Jessy and kept asking her to leave. She kept threatening to turn her in to the next investigator who showed up asking about her. What the heck was her name? Anyway, she and Jessy had a very entertaining hair pulling encounter once. Everyone watched it for a while, laughing mostly, before it got a little too, uh, violent, I'd guess you'd say. When one of them picked up a rock, they stopped it. After that they were at each other all the time."

"Meaning?"

"You know, catty comments. Gossip about each other. Little by little, the whole group, both sects if you will, split off and went away. Tim Brown and I went off one day to Florida, or so we thought. We never made it but ended up buzzing around the South until I'd had enough and decided to go home. David and Cynthia actually made it to Florida. I don't know what happened to them afterward. They always talked about living on a boat, like a houseboat, in the Caribbean. I hope they made it."

"Timothy passed away, you know."

"Yes, I read it in one of Lourdes' newsletters."

"And Jessica stayed behind at the camp?"

"When I left, she had no plans I knew of to leave. Three kids were left from the other group, and two of them swore they were leaving soon. I don't know if they did. The third kid left behind was the one Jessy fought with. I think she and Jessy were too stubborn to be driven out by the other one, but I didn't see them peacefully coexisting as the final two at the camp. They would have killed one another." She chuckled as if she weren't being serious, but when she said it, I got a chill.

"Do you remember the name of the other girl; the one Jessy didn't get along with?"

Shelley pursed her lips. "Now, I'm thinking, I don't know if she ever had a name." She closed her eyes and looked upward.

"Could she have been called Sparkle?"

"Sparkle! Yes, of course. I'm right. She never *did* have a name. I didn't carouse with the other group much. I don't think I remember any of their names but Sparkle. That's something you don't forget, even though it seems I did," she added with a chuckle. "I haven't gone back over this stuff in my mind for years. Sparkle. She was anything but sparkly. Now you've jogged me. I remember her being hostile and keeping mostly to her own group. Really hated it when we all had to lie for Jessy. But I already told you that. She kept in occasional contact with her family to keep them from worrying and coming to look for her."

"And you never got a final report about who stayed in the logging camp?"

"Who would give it to me? Tim and I separated after a month. He went off with me for one reason only, but we don't have to talk about that. I finally came home after the four or five years you mentioned, and I was glad to get there. So were my parents. They never seemed to hold it against me. They were simply happy to have me back with them again. I returned to school and got my high school equivalency diploma. Then I went to BMCC and got a two-year degree, and now, here I am, married, a mom, and working for American Express. Tragedy with a happy ending."

BMCC was a community college across the street from Stuyvesant.

I stood. "You've been very helpful."

She shook her head. "It was a crazy time. Oh, please, I don't have any desire to reconnect with Jessy, so..." She shook her head and waved a finger my way.

"As you wish. I don't think you'd recognize her anyway. She's changed a lot. Tattoos, piercings everywhere."

"My goodness. I'll look at a photo of her, if it would help, but I don't want to see anyone from that time."

"Understood. Thanks again."

"How are you getting back to Manhattan?"

"Taxi?"

"You'd better let me call you a car service. Don't forget, you're out here in the wilds of Staten Island." She offered a friendly smile, and I gladly took her up on her offer. As I rode back to the office, I couldn't get Shelley's words about Sparkle and Jessica out of my mind.

The third kid left behind was the one Jessy fought with. I think she and Jessy were too stubborn to be driven out by the other one, but I didn't see them peacefully coexisting as the final two at the camp. They would have killed one another.

~ * ~

I hung around in the office until a little after six o'clock, reading and drinking coffee. Nothing happened, so I went home. Susan had been sent by the *Post* to Albany, a trip she loathed, to deal with the governor's agenda. She'd be back Sunday, and we planned to meet in Giandos for dinner. I was about to melt some provolone onto a thick slice of tomato and slip it between the halves of a toasted sesame bagel—one of my favorite light dinners—when Henny called.

"How was your interview?" he asked after we'd gotten the greetings out of the way. I told Henny about Shelley's appraisal of Jessica and Sparkle.

"Hmmm," he mused. "Adds a dimension, doesn't it?"

"Sure does."

"I'll keep it in mind. I have a meeting tomorrow morning with a Sergeant Pollard, one of Cotters Grove's finest. So far, I've only talked to him over the phone, but he sounded enthused by the topic. I suppose he doesn't have a lot to do up here."

"Enthused? How so?"

"He must be an older fellow because he remembered the incident. He was on the force at the time. He told me nothing like it has happened since."

"No more bodies found in the woods?"

"Two hunting accidents. Guys got shot by their hunting partner. Nothing suspicious. One died; one survived. He said they were the only notable crimes, if they were crimes, which they were judged not to be, in the past fifteen plus years. I'll know more about what he thinks of the Jessica incident after I talk to him. Looks like I'll be driving back Saturday morning, get home Sunday. I'll be in touch."

I wished him happy hunting, but I don't think he got the meager joke. I didn't think much of it myself.

Since I had the case on my mind, I thought a call to Mr. Towers would at least keep him from interrupting my evening. He listened to my retelling of Shelley's Mak's narrative.

"Concentrate on that angle," he advised. "Question Jessica, if she is Jessica..." Towers usually appended his little 'if she is Jessica' whenever he used her name... "and see if she tells the truth about this Sparkle girl. Get her into your office tomorrow and let me know how she reacts."

I kicked myself for maneuvering myself into this assignment from Towers, but I had no choice but to compliment his cleverness. I took advantage of his approval of my taking his advice by asking whether his promise to cover expenses on top of the big fee he gave us still stood. He assured me it did.

"If your partner manages to confirm Jessica's death, if she is Jessica, let me know immediately. I got a call today from a lawyer she hired. We're meeting on Tuesday, after he meets with Jessica on Monday, so there isn't much time. Work quickly."

I assured him we would, hung up, and went back to my provolone, tomato, and bagel.

Sixteen

When I reached the office next morning, the only person I could think of contacting was Rafael's pal Lourdes Gonzalez. I gave Rafael a call and got her contact information. Rafael cautioned me, in a humorous way that I should have taken more seriously, that Lourdes liked to talk. She turned out to be as eager to chat as Winnie-the-Pooh was to sample honey. Not a very elegant comparison, I admit, but accurate.

Lourdes, it appeared, had not done as well as most other Stuyvesant grads. She lived downtown in the Alfred E. Smith projects, a cluster of seven or eight buildings maybe twenty-five stories high near the Brooklyn Bridge. Smith was a long-ago governor of New York who ran for president in 1928 and lost. He was replaced in the governorship by Franklin Roosevelt, who ran for president the next time around in 1932 and did better than Smith—about four times better. At any rate, the building she lived in had no doorman, so, unchallenged, I took the elevator to the twelfth floor, knocked on her door and identified myself. I'd called ahead and she expected me.

Personally, we matched each other in height, and her curly hair was gathered into a thick, ponytail. When she smiled, not only did I get a display of her teeth but also a decent amount of upper gum came into view. A two-tone smile if you will. It didn't appeal to me.

"Oh, Mr. Lloyd, please come in." The apartment was neat and nicely furnished. "Please, sit." She gestured to a sofa covered in clear plastic, in front of which was a coffee table, where sat four Stuyvesant yearbooks. "I made cookies and tea. Sit, relax. I'll only be a minute. Feel free to look through the yearbooks. I know you'll find them exciting."

I recognized the edition Henny had absconded with from the Stuyvesant library. I knew the kids who'd run away wouldn't be in the next year's book of seniors, so I started paging through the book of their sophomore year. I ran my finger along the list of names under each class photo, and before Lourdes returned with the cookies and tea, I'd found Jessica, David, Cynthia, Shelley from Staten Island, Timothy and Rafael. I don't know what good it did me to find them, except to see that they hadn't yet reached their breaking point with the older generation. On the phone earlier, Lourdes said I'd find a visit with her interesting. When she set the tea and cookies in from of me, I asked what she meant.

"I meant showing you the yearbooks. You found them exciting, didn't you?"

"Yes, yes. Indeed, I did."

"And I can give you access to the newsletters I've written over the years. As someone interested in the Stuyvesant lifestyle, I know you'll find them fascinating." She said this with enthusiasm and a wide, two-tone smile. I didn't have the heart or courage to tell her I had as much interest in the Stuyvesant lifestyle as I had in learning about dental surgery. But to be honest, she did provoke a question in my mind.

"Lourdes, were there other instances of students dropping out of Stuyvesant and running away, disappearing?"

Lourdes' smile faded as the pride she exhibited at being part of the Stuyvesant family came under attack from me. Or so I guessed.

"Well, well, there were always students who couldn't make the grade. The work was difficult and demanding. There were dropouts, of course, of people who didn't measure up. That was to be expected. Don't you agree?"

"Oh, sure. Absolutely." I hadn't meant to put her on the defensive. I merely wondered whether dropping out and running away was a Stuyvesant tradition. A cool thing to do.

"I'm glad you do. The disappearance of five students, some of them still missing to this day... nothing like that had ever happened before or, to my knowledge, since. Everyone, practically everyone in Stuy, came from good families, families to whom education was important. More than important. Paramount."

She went on a while longer defending the Stuyvesant ethos and ended with asking whether I'd like to look over her newsletters. I declined but to prevent her from feeling bad, I did say I'd like to see the one where she reported the death of Jessica Goldman. She brightened up at my request and got a copy out of her files.

"It is with great sadness that I report the death of one of our family. Jessica Goldman has passed away while visiting in Maine. Despite her shortened stay in Stuy (she dropped out during her junior year) I'm sure many of you remember her with great love and affection."

"I kept the announcement short and dignified, don't you think?" Lourdes asked, a plea for approval beaming from her eyes.

"You struck the perfect tone. I commend you," I offered back. A bright smile returned to her face and now, having returned her to the happy condition in which I'd found her, I got up from the sofa. "I must get back to my office. May I take a couple?" I asked, reaching for two cookies. "Homemade, aren't they?"

"Yes, I'm so glad you like them. Would you care to be put on my mailing list for Stuy information?"

My head said no thank you, but my heart said, "I'd appreciate that." I gave her the office email address and made my escape, promising myself I'd take very seriously any further character sketches Rafael Wallingford provided to me.

The afternoon held nothing more of interest outside of calls from Jessica and Reginald Towers, both asking the same question. Had Henny and I made any progress? Both mentioned the upcoming meeting on Tuesday with Jessica's new lawyer in attendance. I could only answer that Henny was hard at work in Maine, and I was doing what I could here in the city. Neither one seemed satisfied with my answer and a little after five, I went home to my lonely Brooklyn apartment, first stopping at Henny's and my favorite liquor store to take home a bottle of *Boone's That's All Whiskey*. I wouldn't be so lonely after all.

When I woke up later than usual Saturday morning, I was surprised Henny hadn't called. Or maybe he had, and I missed it, but no, when I checked my cell, no calls had come in. The interview with Lourdes Gonzalez hadn't given me anything worth passing along to Henny, and I felt at a loss at how to spend the day. I wandered into the office around noon feeling useless. Not a single worthwhile investigatory activity crossed my mind. If I were a betting man, I'd bet on Jessica Goldman actually being Jessica Goldman. I envisaged Reginald Towers crumbling on Tuesday under dire threats from Jessica's lawyers and handing over ten million dollars on the spot.

An hour later, for no reason I can think of, I recalled my mother having a footprint of mine made at the hospital when I was born. I didn't know whether to call Mr. Towers with a suggestion to look for a thirty-eight-year-old baby footprint of Jessica's or not. It sounded frivolous when I said it out loud, but if one existed, it could be determinative. I finally decided to hold onto my idea and spring it if all else failed.

Scars, moles, beauty marks—did Jessica have any? Both Mr. Towers and Jessica would have brought them up if there were any. Of course, Mr. Towers wouldn't be up to date on body marks on Jessica, or, at least, he shouldn't be, but Jessica would. What, though, would she have to compare them against? Finally, since I was getting nowhere, I thought I might as well spend the afternoon at the movies, then maybe pass the evening at the bar in Giandos. I occasionally got a good idea staring through Giandos' floor to ceiling windows into Manhattan from my seat at the bar. Maybe I'd get one tonight.

Fortunately, the good idea came from hundreds of miles north. As I sat at my desk deciding between a movie and going home for a nap, Henny called on the landline.

"Hey," I greeted, "what's up?"

"Lloyd, this may turn out to be the best trip ever. You won't believe it. Sergeant Pollard is my new best friend, no offense."

"No, no. None taken. Explain."

"I mentioned to you he was on the force back when someone found so-called Jessica's body in the woods."

"You did."

"According to Pollard, there were five officers on the entire force back then."

"How many now?"

"Looks like maybe twenty or so. They have computers and every modern convenience. Anyway, there's a basement here at the Cotters Grove police station. A dark and dusty basement, according to Pollard, where they store stuff."

"What kind of stuff?"

"Stuff from previous cases. Pollard tells me there's not an awful lot that's been worth saving, the crime rate in Cotters Grove being on the low side, but he doesn't see any reason they haven't saved the physical evidence from Jessica's demise—he thinks he remembers they did at the time— and if it survived, it would be in the basement."

"Did you look?"

"Pollard is running around looking for the basement key. This place isn't organized under the tightest protocols. He promised if he didn't find the key, we'd remove the basement door. So, we'll get down there sooner or later."

"Well, I guess that's good news. I told you about the meeting of Jessica's lawyer and Mr. Towers this Tuesday, didn't I?" I quickly mentioned the useless meeting with Lourdes.

"You did mention the meeting. I expect to be home early Monday. I'll keep you informed. Oh, Pollard just walked into the door waving a key at me. Gotta go!"

A portion of my useless feeling evaporated. Henny and Lloyd were on the job. At least Henny was. I decided to go home and nap, then Giandos, then a relaxing stretch until I met Susan, hoping all the while to hear some good news from Henny.

~ * ~

Henny called on Saturday evening to report that he and Pollard had found what they were looking for in a spidery, dank corner of the police station basement, and they were waiting for test results from the state capital, the name of which neither he nor I knew. I looked it up later. Augusta.

"But I had an insight," Henny crowed. "You wouldn't believe the insight I had."

"You're repeating yourself. What was this great insight? And what kind of tests?"

"Nope, not now. I want to know it turned out all right and solved the case. That's why we're waiting to hear from the capital."

"Solved the case! Was it Jessica or Sparkle or someone else they found in the woods?"

"Gotta go. What time is the Tuesday meeting?"

"I don't know."

"Find out and let me know. Tell them you and I may be attending."

"Why..." I began, but Henny ended the call.

I texted Reginald Towers and asked for details of Tuesday's meeting. One o'clock in his office at Twenty-third Street and Fifth Avenue. I texted the information along to Henny but got no response. I imagined him deep into his insight.

Sunday night when I met Susan in Giandos, she brought me up to speed on the governor's doings, and I shared with her what little I'd uncovered about the Jessica Goldman inheritance.

"Henny's keeping you in suspense about his case-breaking insight?"

"He is. He sounded excited, though. Considering where he was when he left town, deep in the depths of a broken heart, I heard a great improvement."

"Well, insight or not, at least that sounds like good news. You or me?" Susan was referring to the notification sound on our phones.

"Me, I think." I checked. "Yeah." I stared at the message Henny had sent and read it twice.

"What?" Susan asked, staring my way.

"Henny. I quote: 'Hard evidence Jessica is really Jessica. More to look into, though. I'll be in touch. Won't be back Monday but will certainly see you at the Tuesday meeting. Maybe big news. We'll see.'"

"Wow," Susan said in a whisper. "The moment you leave that meeting on Tuesday, you call me. I want to know exactly what went on."

"I will. I will."

Susan left after our dinner on Sunday, claiming she had a million things to do at home, and I went to bed and tossed and turned, running through possible scenarios for Tuesday's meeting. Henny had found a cozy spot in my head and wouldn't leave. I hoped he wasn't building us up for a great fall. Henny had great detective radar, though. Finally, tired of having Henny on my mind, I replaced him with Susan and slept much better afterwards.

I heard nothing from anyone on Monday and spent the day in the office reading one of Henny's 1940s' mysteries and, back in my apartment as the evening deepened, sipping some *Boone's That's All Whiskey*. I slept quite soundly that night.

Seventeen

I always silence the notifications alert on my phone when I tuck myself in for the night, so when I awoke on Tuesday morning and checked my phone, I saw a text Henny had sent an hour earlier. It said he was leaving his motel and would see me in Jessica's lawyer's office, and I shouldn't forget to inform Mr. Towers that he would be there. If he ran into traffic and was late, I should delay the meeting for as long as I could. He must have something, I thought to myself. Maybe.

I saw no reason to go to Centre Street and the office since I couldn't think of anything to do there and didn't want a new case intruding on my day. The one o'clock meeting still hours away, I returned to my bed and closed my eyes. I didn't get very far because Susan called me fifteen minutes later.

"I didn't wake you, did I?" she asked. "I didn't get an answer on your office phone."

If people who said, "I didn't wake you, did I?" were truly concerned with awakening their call recipient, they wouldn't call, would they? But I didn't offer that little nugget of wisdom to Susan.

"No, I was up. I got a text from Henny, and he's still on the road and will meet me at the lawyer's office."

"Did he say anything about his insight?"

"He did not."

"Okay. I called you to remind you to call me first thing afterward."

"Susan, of course I will."

"Okay, you can go back to sleep now."

"What? How did you know...?"

"Bye."

Henny and Susan both seemed to doubt my ability to remember things. And how did she know I planned to go back to sleep? Susan had many mysterious qualities. I gave Mr. Towers a quick call to be certain things were on schedule. They were. Then I cleared my mind and drifted off till noon.

~ * ~

Except for Henny, everyone appeared on time in Reginald Towers' office, Jessica likely setting off any metal detector she'd come within shouting distance of. A droopy nose ring; something through her lower lip she hadn't worn around me before; the usual line of metal studs down each ear, and patches of dark blue tattoo ink on any exposed skin. After we arranged ourselves around a rectangular desk, me sitting directly across from Jessica, one lawyer at each end of the table, introductions went round, and I learned the name of Jessica's lawyer was Charles Trevor, midthirties, and overly well-groomed—his hair could have been used as a TV commercial for anything involving beautiful male hair. He worked hard and successfully, I might add, to give the impression of being a no-nonsense, don't-mess-with-me lawyer. He commandeered the meeting right off.

"I'd first like to know why this gentleman is here." Trevor indicated me.

Towers defended me. "He is one of the two private investigators I've hired to get to the truth. His partner will be joining us."

"His partner! Where is he? Why isn't he here?" Trevor demanded.

I answered. "Henny spent the last few days in Maine, the town of Cotters Grove, where the supposed death of Jessica Goldman took place. He is returning with important information."

I presumed that was what Henny was returning with. My stomach performed a small lurch when I noticed Jessica react to my comment. Her brow wrinkled and she bit her lower lip for a moment. "If we could wait until he arrives, I'm sure..."

Trevor interrupted. "No, we cannot wait. Everyone is able to tell time, I presume. And you, Mr. Towers, why the devil are you here? As a named heir in the late Mr. Goldman's will, you're involved in a clear case of conflict of interest. Your interests are directly antagonistic to this woman you've been counseling. Explain yourself." Trevor folded his arms across his chest and sat back.

Towers' nostrils gave a flicker of anger. "Ms. Goldman's interests and mine align exactly. We both want to know the truth of the matter. Ms. Goldman claims she is the previously-thought-dead Jessica, daughter of the deceased, and I wish to prove or disprove the truth of the matter. I contend there is no conflict of interest. Also, I was the first person the alleged Ms. Goldman came to upon her return. It was only natural that she do so. I was close friends with her father, as well as his legal adviser for nearly forty years. Now, let's get down to business. This is not a court of law but an attempt to resolve this situation amicably."

I thought Towers had stretched his explanation embarrassingly thin, but Trevor seemed prepared to go on.

"Hasn't Ms. Goldman stood up to your questioning? She tells me she's answered every question you put to her—and being such a close family acquaintance, you asked numerous questions that only she would know the answer to. Isn't that so?"

"She demonstrated a knowledge of her father and the family, yes."

"'Demonstrated' or shown a *complete* knowledge of her family's history?" Trevor sat in silence waiting for Towers' answer. Finally, he got it.

"With ten million dollars at stake, I believe we need more. We need absolute, conclusive evidence."

Trevor gave a sarcastic chuckle. "You try that tack in front of a judge, and he'll hand you a pen to write out Ms. Goldman's check."

Towers bristled some but didn't respond. Trevor, though, kept going.

"If you are not satisfied with Ms. Goldman's account and demonstrable knowledge of what surely proves her identity, then we have no choice but to go forward with a court case, at which I will argue that you, Mr. Towers, have no place." Slowly he added, "Because of a raging conflict of interest."

We endured maybe ninety seconds of silence before the door opened, and Henny entered the room, dressed in his usual dark pinstriped suit and black fedora. Today's hat had no little feather in it, Henny's sense of propriety being spot on.

He took the chair next to me and laid his hat on the table. I saw him eye a metal coat rack in the corner of the room, but thankfully, his hat stayed where it lay. When I'd turned at the sound of Henny opening the door, not only did I see Henny enter, but through the doorway I saw another figure I recognized. Detective Thursday from the NYPD. "Good morning, everyone," Henny greeted from his seat. Thursday remained in the waiting room.

We sat through another round of introductions, after which Trevor attempted to reestablish control. "And what, may I ask, is the purpose of your being here?"

It now became Henny's show. He ran his eyes across each person in the room, then said, "I've just arrived from a trip to Cotters Grove, Maine. You are familiar with Cotters Grove, aren't you, Ms. Goldman."

"Yes, I am. And Jessica, please."

"Jessica, yes. I can advise this group that the likelihood of you being the person you claim to be is undeniable." Jessica made a fist and gave it a mini-pump as Henny continued. "I can say this because, without question, the dead girl found those many years ago has been positively identified. She was a runaway young woman known as Sparkle but her given name is... was... Vicky Trilby. She was born and grew up in Ohio and, like your friends and yourself, Jessica, she ran away at a young age and ended up at the logging camp outside of Cotters Grove."

Trevor interrupted. "That's great news and good work on your part, sir. Mr. Towers, I suggest..."

Henny interrupted right back. "I've not finished. Calm down."

Trevor paused, chastened, I thought, by Henny's snap back. "Go on," Trevor said.

"We know who Vicky Trilby is because... well, let me back up, first. The body was presumed to be you, Jessica. You claimed..." Here Henny looked at me, and I gave him an encouraging nod. "...Vicky was a thief and stole your things, and the only identification found on her indicated she was you. There was minimal damage to her body, even though the authorities think she may have lain in the woods for two or three days before she was found. Since there were no photographs available and since it seemed you and she were the final two people to leave the camp, the authorities—basically a five-man police force—decided that the identification found on her was enough. It was Jessica Goldman who had died, and so, in time, they contacted your father. But now we know it wasn't you."

"I told you she was a thief," Jessica said.

Henny rapped on the table once. "I'm not finished. No, it appears she was *not* a thief."

Jessica stared at him. "Excuse me?" she said.

"I said Vicky Tilly was not a thief."

"What are you getting at?" Trevor asked. "Ms. Goldman's story holds true at every point."

"No, it doesn't. The Cotters Grove police may not have done a great job on the case overall—only a bunch of annoying kids camping out in the woods—but at least they saved the evidence from the incident: a leather wallet, a silver pen, and a small, blank notebook with a plastic cover. These three items were covered with matching fingerprints, obviously, to the police, the dead girl's. So, the Cotters Grove police closed the case. If they'd investigated a little further... but they didn't.

"Looking over the evidence this past week on the presumption that the body did *not* belong to Jessica and with Jessica's story of Sparkle as a thief caused a problem to arise. Why were there no fingerprints from Sparkle on those items?" Henny cast his gaze around the table. "The Cotters Grove police assumed the fingerprints were those of the person the items were found on. But since we clearly know they did not belong to Sparkle, how did she acquire them without touching them. How did she get them into her pockets without leaving her fingerprints on them? Gloves would be the only way, but the idea of gloves is preposterous. For one thing, it was summer. The items were supposedly stolen from indoors, and even if it was a cold summer day, no gloves were found anywhere near the body or anywhere inside any of the cabins where the runaways stayed at the time. The Cotters Grove police did manage to search the logging camp, if they did little enough else." Henny waited a moment before saying, "Any ideas, Jessica?"

"I... I... I don't know. I only know she was a thief and took my stuff."

"No, it's clear she wasn't a thief. Someone planted those things on her body. There was one set of surprise fingerprints, though.

Sparkle, Vicky Trilby, wore a small medal, well, a little bigger than a medal but not so large as a medallion, around her neck."

I noticed a twitch in Jessica's eyelids and the tip of her tongue ran across her lips.

"Sparkle's fingerprints were on the medal, but so were yours, Jessica. They exactly matched the fingerprints on the other evidence. How did your fingerprints get on Sparkle's medal?"

Silence ensued for a count of maybe fifty.

"Jessica?" Henny prodded.

"No way," Jessica burst out. "There's a mistake."

"You and she didn't get along," Henny said, keeping his eyes fixed on Jessica. "So, I doubt you shared fashion accessories, true?"

Anger crossed Jessica's face.

"Your fingerprint got onto the medal when you... what? Strangled her? Fought with her that last day? Try to remember."

"No, no. What are you talking about? She no doubt stole the medal from me. Yes, that had to be it. She stole my medal. That's how her fingerprint got on it."

Henny took a deep breath. "Her fingerprint got on the medal but on nothing else she had with her? Can you remember what was on the medal?"

"Not really. Some design, I think."

"No," Henny responded. "It had 5/18/88 engraved on one side and the letters V. T. on the side. Vicky's birthdate and initials. We identified Vicky through an FBI database for persons reported missing during the months of September and October, 2009. Vicky, not quite the rebel you were, Jessica, contacted her parents in some manner once a month, give or take, to let them know she was well. Her mother is still alive, and we spoke with her. When her daughter failed to contact the family for the entire summer of 2009, her parents reported her missing and gave the FBI some of her things, from which they lifted fingerprints. The fingerprints on file for her matched the fingerprint which wasn't yours on the medal.

A facial photo Vicky's mother provided matched a photo taken of the corpse."

Henny took a deep breath. "So, Jessica, if you claim the medal was yours, we're left with asking you why you would have a medal bearing Vicky's initials and birthdate. She seemed never to remove the medal since she was wearing it even in the photo her mother provided to the FBI. You planted those items with your fingerprints and name on Vicky's body after... After what, Jessica?"

"This is crazy," Jessica said, getting to her feet. "Mr. Trevor, how can you allow this?"

For once, Trevor had no answer.

Henny said, "I have a friend in the other room." He got to his feet and went to the door and beckoned. "This is Detective Thursday from the New York Police Department. He's been in contact with Inspector Pollard from Cotters Grove. Cotters Grove would like you back, Jessica. They believe you had something to do with Vicky's death, or rather, her murder."

"What!" Jessica shrieked. "There's a statute of limitations. It's way long ago. I don't have to go back anywhere."

Thursday gestured at the open doorway to the next room, and two other gentlemen in police uniforms stepped into the conference room, and Jessica slumped back in her chair.

Trevor cleared his throat and said, "Do you have a warrant..."

Detective Thursday already had a folded paper out of his inside pocket and held it in the air.

"Care to take a look?" he asked Trevor, who made his way, an embarrassed look on his face, to where Thursday stood. He glanced quickly at the warrant and returned it to Thursday.

"It's a legal warrant," he said to Jessica before returning to his end of the table.

The meeting broke up, Jessica being escorted out by the men in blue. Thursday shook Henny's hand and thanked him.

"Good news for you, it seems," I said to Towers.

"Why doesn't it feel like good news?" he said. "Do you think she actually murdered that girl?"

Henny answered. "She practically confessed right here. Statute of limitations?" He shook his head. "Not for murder."

A subdued Reginald Towers said, "Keep me up to date on anything I should know. Oh, submit your expenses to my office, and I'll see to them."

We shook hands all around and left.

Eighteen

The first thing I did when Henny and I got back to our office was to call Susan. I filled her in and readily admit to sharing in the excitement she demonstrated. Her tone told me everything. This could be a great story, she said, and I pictured her jumping up and down, clapping her hands—something she'd never do, but that's the image that popped up. She said she would head to Detective Thursday's office as soon as she finished the weird story (her words) she was currently working on. It became my turn to extract a promise to be kept up to date.

Henny sat at his desk, having finished retrieving his fedora from the floor after he'd missed flinging it to a happy landing onto the coat rack arm for the seven millionth time, according to my count. He'd filled me in on as much as he could on the fifteen-minute cab ride from Reginald Towers' office.

"So, you had a memorable trip, eh?" I said, returning my attention to my partner.

"Incredible. And I've saved the best of the story till right now. Ready?"

"Ready."

"The insight... the moment of the insight. I never believed it when it happened in the books I read. You've read a lot of them, too. The detective is sitting there thinking or doing nothing whatever, and then he jumps up and says, 'I've solved it!' Some little thing sets off a chain reaction in his brain, and like those dominoes that fall over in a line... BAM! He's got the solution! It always seemed to me that the author simply wanted to go home early, but now I know it happens because it happened to me! Pollard and I were looking over the stuff we found in the box marked J. Goldman. When I saw the leather and the plastic—*fingerprints* jumped into my head, and just like that, the first domino fell. Chain reaction underway. I looked over the written reports—the fingerprints were all the same on the leather and plastic. Can you believe the five officers at the time didn't have the brains to match the fingerprints on the evidence with the deceased's actual fingerprints. Pollard remembers they just carted the body to the funeral parlor."

"Maybe *they* wanted to go home early."

"Yeah, really! Pollard told me they made the assumption the stuff found in Vicky Trilby's pockets belonged to Vicky Trilby aka Jessica Goldman. Case closed. But one line at the bottom of the report noted an odd fingerprint on the medal she wore. It didn't match the others. So, two people. If Sparkle stole the stuff from Jessica, as she told us Sparkle did, Jessica's prints would naturally be all over the leather and plastic... but... where were the thief's fingerprints? Where were Sparkle's fingerprints? Boom! Fireworks in my brain. We sent the one odd fingerprint to the FBI and asked them to check the missing persons of twenty-ish years old who were reported missing September or October 2009, and bingo! Sparkle's mother had sent something with her daughter's fingerprint as well as a photo of her to them, and they matched it.

Pretty easy to put things together after that. The two girls didn't like one another, and Jessica killed Sparkle and planted her IDs to get her father off her back and continue life free as a bird. Case solved and from *my* insight!"

"Wow, real detective work. We need to buy a sign that reads INSIGHT and hang it on our wall."

"I wouldn't complain."

Happily, it was clear to me Henny had put the Daria Givens episode behind.

I offered to buy Henny dinner at Bocca di Bacco, but he preferred to go home and catch up on his rest. If he never drove again to Maine, he said, it would be too soon for him.

~ * ~

The next morning, I grabbed a *New York Post* on the way to the office and scanned the first few pages. On page three I saw Susan's name under the headline:

RETURN FROM THE DEAD

Susan had the facts and added that Jessica Goldman had retained lawyers who were plea- bargaining for all they were worth. I saw Reginald Towers' hand in this. With his likely million-dollar inheritance looming, he could afford to send some lawyers Jessica's way.

Susan called a few minutes after I plopped down in my desk chair, coffee in hand.

"Did you see my story?"

"I did. Great stuff. I picked up the *Post* on the way in and read your story on the train. Great headline. Yours?"

"Ha! No. At the *Post* somebody gets paid to think up wild headlines. I guess he earned his week's pay with that one."

"I guess he did. When will I see you?"

"If you're not busy..."

"Don't rub it in."

Susan chuckled. "You just nailed a big case. You saw your names in print, right?"

"I did, and we thank you."

"I was saying, if you're not busy, I'll stop by in the afternoon. Henny there yet?"

"Nope."

"He should hear this too."

"Hear what?"

"You don't need me to tell it twice. Wild, crazy story. You'll love it. Gotta go. Love you."

"Love you, too. Bye."

She hung up and left me in suspense, like any good writer should.

When Henny arrived, we went over the Jessica Goldman case for a while then settled into our usual routine, me reading, this time a Nero Wolfe novel my partner had passed on to me, and Henny fiddling with his unending supply of toothpicks. I offered to make a trip to Chinatown and celebrate his recent detection insight by treating him to his favorite, moo shu pork, and received a brisk thumbs up. When I got back to the office, Susan sat in our client chair, and I generously shared my pancakes with her.

Susan and Henny laughed about something while I cleaned up after lunch. I interrupted their jollity and asked, "What's this crazy thing you have to tell us?"

I settled into my desk chair as Susan pulled two business cards from her purse and handed one to Henny and the other to me. Mine read, "Doctor So Yen Chung, Eastern Transcendentalist." A web address as well as an email address and a Greenwich Village address filled the bottom corners of the card.

"Doctor Chung?" I asked, turning to Henny.

He lifted the card. "The very same."

"Who is he?" I asked Susan.

"Aside from being an Eastern Transcendentalist?"

"Yes."

"He's a mystic who successfully foretells the future."

"Successfully?" I repeated.

"Successfully. Want to hear?"

"You know I do."

"Ha, ha. Very funny. Doctor Chung is Asian, as you may have deduced. He wanders around Lower Manhattan and the Village and reveals to some lucky person his or her future."

"While walking around?" Henny asked.

"Pretty much. He has recently, though, opened a place in the Village. The address is on the card. But to the point, there are six verifiable instances of him approaching random people and correctly predicting something that would happen to them later in the day. He foretold added wealth three times, and it came true; twice through the person finding a wallet with a little money in it and once finding a lottery ticket worth twenty bucks when the fellow checked it at the convenience store."

"And you know this how?" I asked.

"The good doctor gave each of these people a card like the one you're holding. Word got around."

"What about the other three people?" Henny asked.

"Same thing but different. No money involved. Once he predicted a moment of danger, and the fellow received a glancing touch from a careless driver, who then sped away. Another man was warned not to travel down a particular street, which happened to be the street he lived on. He ignored the doctor and got mugged."

"How was he supposed to get home?" Henny asked.

"He was told not to walk down the street. Should have taken a cab, I guess," Susan said.

"And one more?" I added.

"Yes, the man was told he would soon receive a special gift. The next day in the mail came two anonymous tickets to a Yankees game in September. As I mentioned, word spread about the prescient doctor. I interviewed Dr. Chung at his newly opened place of business and got a lot of mumbo jumbo about Transcendentalism, which made very little sense to me. Simply put, he calls it the knowledge of what is and will be."

"Whatever that means," Henny mumbled. "Did he tell your future?"

"No. I didn't request it and don't want to know." Susan smiled my way. "It would prevent Lloyd from ever surprising me."

"And what's the bottom line of this story?" I asked. I figured Susan had a point to make.

"He's set up shop in a storefront on MacDougal Street. He's gotten enough notoriety that now, people come to him."

"To have their futures told?" I asked. "People actually believe he can do this stuff?"

"Some people will believe anything," Susan said, smiling. "He's charging a good fee, five hundred dollars a session, and people do show up. When I interviewed him, I had to cut our conversation short because he had a client in fifteen minutes and needed to clear his mind, so he said. This was a week ago. I left but I waited outside and kept watch. I saw an older woman go in and thirty minutes later, a happier older woman come out. I introduced myself to her and asked if she'd seen Doctor Chung. She was indeed his client, and she told me that he foresaw a man, a *new* man—her emphasis—entering her life. She positively glowed as she walked away."

"Can I presume she isn't married?" Henny asked.

"You can. She told me the reason she visited Doctor Chung was to learn if something like that was possible again for her. Doctor Chung assured her it was. I gave her my card and asked her to keep me up to date. Just three days ago, she called and told me she'd met the most wonderful gentleman, a fellow named Leonard, Leonard Faraday. Doctor Chung possessed the power he claimed to have, she assured me. She hoped to schedule another session with Chung to ask whether she had a marriage in her future."

"And he charges five hundred bucks for this claptrap?" Henny said, frowning. "Aiming for a certain high-level clientele, it seems."

"Five hundred bucks is a big bite," I said softly.

"Why are you telling us this?" Henny asked.

"It's got to be a scam," Susan argued. "Don't you see? I smell a good story in there somewhere."

"Pointing out how stupid people can be?" Henny asked.

"Nobody's hired Henny and me to do anything about it," I pointed out. "We work for a living."

"I know. I know," Susan said. "I just... it's, I don't know. It doesn't sit right with me. I'm going to look into this Doctor Chung, starting with Ms. Gladys Rutherford, the lady with the new boyfriend. Something shady's going on. Gotta be. Maybe I can get the Rutherford woman to hire you."

"To do what?" Henny asked.

"To check out the mystical Dr. Chung. What else? What do you say?"

Henny and I exchanged glances, and I shrugged. "Okay with me. If she's willing to fork over five hundred dollars on nonsense like learning the future, she should be willing to fork out for us."

Henny gave me a look.

"That didn't come out right," I admitted. "You know what I mean. She'll pay."

"I hope so," Henny agreed, and the conversation drifted on to other things.

~ * ~

That evening around nine, Henny texted me he was coming to visit. A short trip of three floors upward had him on my sofa in a few minutes. He carried a book in his hand.

"Giving me another classic 1940s' *noir* adventure?" I asked, handing him a short *Boone's That's All Whiskey*. "I didn't finish with Nero Wolfe yet."

He waved his free hand negatively. "No, no. Here, see?" He held the book up so I could read the title. *The Future Unfurled.*

I stared for a quiet instant. "And?"

"I've been reading it. Here, look. The author."

Printed in smaller letters under the title was the name So Yen Chung.

"That's the name Susan gave us."

"I know. I know," Henny went on with a spirit in his voice he didn't usually exhibit. "It says inside that it's translated from the Chinese. The introduction claims the book was originally printed in 1946 and has only recently been turned into English—in 1967."

"Recently?"

"Recently when this edition was printed."

"Where'd you get it?"

"It was in my bookcase, believe it or not. I don't remember where I got it. Probably for a quarter at an old book sale. I didn't even know I had it until I happened to catch the title in a random glance. Then I saw the author's name."

Henny gave me a look as if he expected me to respond, but I could come up with nothing more profound than, "And?"

"The name of the author. Same as Susan's guy."

I shook my head. "I know the book's being originally published in the forties is a strong recommendation for you, but the guy who wrote it back then would have to be over a hundred years old by now. Longevity *and* fortune-telling would be a bit over the top, don't you think?"

Henny frowned, shook his head, and muttered, "No, no, no. Of course, not the same man, but a relative? Son, grandson in on the family secret?"

I shrugged my dubious opinion. "Did you read the book? What's it say?"

"I read some. It claims that the future is happening right this minute, only we can't see it."

"But the Chung family can?"

"With training, this Doctor Chung..." Henny tapped his book. "...assures his readers that he can see what no one else can. There's got to be some connection between the two Doctor Chungs."

"And our interest in this is what?"

Henny looked abashed. "Well, nothing yet, I suppose. But what a coincidence, eh? It's like something out there is telling us to take a look into the Chung phenomenon."

"Chung phenomenon, eh? And what something would be sending us this message?"

"How do I know?" Henny nearly yelled. "Things like this don't just happen."

"Were you sipping on some *Boone's* while you were reading?"

"Maybe. A little." He tossed back what was remaining in the glass I'd given him. "Call Susan. Tell her about the book. See what she says. No way she won't be interested."

I felt reluctant to join Henny in his airy world of "something out there is telling us to take a look" but to be honest, he had a point about Susan. Not only Susan; I found it, let's say, odd, and yes, interesting too. I made the call. Susan sounded enthused, and Henny had me promise to give her the book the next time I saw her.

"I'll leave it for you now to read," he said. His excitement hadn't flagged. "It's short. You'll finish before bedtime. Take it to the office tomorrow." Henny got to his feet. "There's something in this..." He shivered his hands next to his head as if he were getting signals from the ether.

"I'll read it," I promised. "And I'll take it with me tomorrow."

After Henny left, I poured myself another short *Boone's* and settled back to see how the Chung family explained their strange ability.

Nineteen

"I want you to come with me," Susan said after greeting me with a quick kiss late the next morning in the office. Her cheeks were a rosy red from the weather, and she looked delicious.

"Come with you where?" I asked. "Sit."

"What about me?" Henny chimed in.

Susan unbuttoned her down jacket and took a seat in our client chair. "To interview Gladys Rutherford."

"You'll introduce me as... a private detective?" I asked.

"Why not? She must have some suspicions about this. She can't be that naïve. I feel comfortable suggesting to her she go slowly with this... charade. I'll use another word, though."

"Maybe she *is* that naïve and *has* no suspicions," Henny added. "She seems to have jumped in neck deep and loves it."

"She's agreed to meet me for lunch today, and she appears to be bubbling over with wanting to talk about her experience."

"She's had the boyfriend for, what, four days?" Henny said. "He must be quite a fellow."

Susan nodded thoughtfully. "I want to get her to tell me as much as she can about this Leonard Faraday. You'll come, Lloyd? Sorry, Henny, I don't want to overwhelm the lady."

"Don't worry. I'll man the fort," Henny promised. "You haven't shown Susan the book."

"I'll come. Sure. Nothing to keep me here. No offense," I offered Henny. "Oh, here." I took the ancient Doctor Chung's book from my top desk drawer.

"It's got a Fu Man Chu look to it," Susan said, paging through the book. "The illustrations."

I turned to Henny. "Fu Man Chu I've heard of. From the forties?"

"A couple of his books were written in the forties, but the first book goes back to the nineteen teens."

"Wow, been around a long time."

"I'll take this with me," Susan said, indicating the book and throwing glances at Henny and me, looking for approval.

"Sure," Henny said. "If you get to talk to the current Doctor Chung again, bring it up, get his reaction. Must be a connection."

"Let's go, lover," Susan said to me. "You and I have a lunch appointment.

~ * ~

Gladys Rutherford looked about fifty years old, maybe a little more. Five foot-six, give or take, well-dressed, laden with jewelry—earrings, three rings on each hand, a shiny silver chain from which a large pearl dangled—she gave the appearance of a rich matron heading toward senior citizenship status. She offered a wide smile when she spotted Susan and gestured graciously to chairs on either side of her at the square table. She'd chosen Chez Maison on West Forty-Seventh street in the theatre district, a darkish establishment three steps below street level. A gas fire burned in what was once a genuine fireplace. All in all, the place felt cozy. I liked it.

"And who is this handsome young man?" Gladys asked, indicating me. She twittered her fingers above her head, and a waiter appeared.

"He's someone I want you to meet," Susan said. We ordered drinks and scanned the menu.

"Is he a good friend of yours?" Gladys asked, an amorous twinkle in her eye. Her recent infatuation having elevated her emotions, she likely had a desire to spread her good fortune to others. She hadn't yet lost her introductory smile.

Susan prepared to drop the other shoe as we ordered lunch and accepted our drinks.

"You can call him Lloyd," Susan said.

"Nice to meet you, Lloyd," Gladys said, extending her hand to me. I took it and reciprocated her opinion about the niceness of our meeting.

"He's a private detective," Susan announced.

Gladys let go of my hand. "A private detective! My goodness." A look of confusion replaced her smile.

Susan dashed ahead. "We'd really like to know more about this man you met."

"I... I don't understand. A private detective?"

"And about Doctor Chung. I've told you some of Chung's history, what little there is to tell," Susan said.

"You have, and I've told you what a wonderful man the doctor is. He knows things. He sees..." She moved her arm through the air, indicating, I suppose, the future. I wondered how Susan would smooth this over. Gladys did not look happy with me.

"You have. And no doubt he is a wonder. That's exactly why I'd like to learn more. You know I write for the *New York Post*. This would be a wonderful story if I knew more about your experience. Imagine the joy and hope Doctor Chung might bring to others just as he's brought them to you."

Gladys settled back a bit, and I owed Susan a compliment later for her fine work calming the woman.

"Yes, yes. I can see that," Gladys agreed. She took a dainty sip of her chardonnay.

Susan went on. "How did you learn about him?"

Gladys glanced at me. "Private detective?" she repeated.

"Lloyd often helps me with my research. He's very talented that way."

I figured I'd better speak up and stop sitting there like a mummy.

"Your experience with Doctor Chung is amazing," I offered. "Susan hasn't stopped talking to me about how impressed she is by the doctor and by you. Your faith in his vision is inspiring." I caught Susan's eye and saw approval in it. "Any way I can help Susan to give a wonderful story like yours to the public would be gratifying, and I'm eager to assist where I can."

A smile crept back on Gladys's face, and our luncheon returned to happier ground.

"I read about him in your newspaper, as a matter of fact," Gladys explained. "Maybe it was even you who wrote the story. It was a short piece."

"I'm sure it was me," Susan agreed. "The story's been mine all along."

"My Charles died two years ago."

"Mr. Rutherford?" Susan asked.

"Yes. It's been a lonely two years. I decided I had nothing to lose, so I went to see Doctor Chung. We spoke and he suggested I return in a week."

"Why two visits?"

"He held my hand for... for at least twenty minutes. We sat quietly for the most part. He asked me some questions—where I lived, my recent history. I was honest with him. He told me he needed to absorb my spirit, to live with my being for a week. He assured me his vision could penetrate my aura, and my future would come clear to him. I want to tell you it was the longest week

I'd ever experienced, but when I returned, he foresaw Leonard entering my life. He knew.He knew."

"Leonard is the man you met, of course."

"Yes. Leonard Farraday. It's scarcely been a week, yet I feel as if I've known Leonard my whole life."

Gladys was off and running about the wonders of Leonard Farraday. A retired worker, no specifics. A fellow of little family, and a hazy past with few highlights.

"You don't know much about him," I put in.

"I know all I need to know. He's kind, gentle, wonderful, attentive." Thankfully, she ran out of adjectives.

"Do you know where he lives?" I asked.

"Somewhere in the thirties on the westside," Gladys answered. "But we don't go there. He comes to my apartment. He seems so happy when he's there."

I didn't doubt it.

"And where do you live?" Susan asked.

"East Thirty-Seventh. Near First Avenue."

She and Susan chatted, and I listened carefully for any nuggets I could pick up about Leonard Faraday. There weren't many. After we'd eaten, Gladys checked her watch.

"I'm meeting Leonard in fifteen minutes right out front." She pointed toward the entrance.

"We'd love to meet him, too," Susan said. "May we?"

"Of course." Gladys giggled. "Don't mention, please, what I told you about my going back to Doctor Chung to ask if marriage is in my future. I don't want to scare Leonard away."

We chuckled in unison and after Susan paid the bill, or more likely after the *Post* paid the bill, we stood in the vestibule of Chez Maison waiting for Leonard to appear.

Gladys bolted out of the restaurant when a rotund man of middle-height dressed in a gray overcoat and a fuzzy, warm hat hove into sight. Susan and I trailed her and paused as the two embraced. When they separated, she escorted Leonard toward us. His cheeks and chin had produced a meager gray stubble, maybe two days' growth. It surprised me he didn't go out of his way to present a better image of himself, considering Gladys's social status. And probably her financial status as well, but as yet, I didn't know to what level that reached. I noticed Leonard's black shoes were scuffed and assumed her finances were in better shape than his. He had a wide and winning smile, though, and beamed it at Susan and me as we were introduced. Gladys did not introduce me as a private detective but rather as a newspaper man.

Leonard's gaze stayed on me as his smile melted, making it clear that he wasn't pleased with this new situation—meaning me—but Gladys rattled on.

"Susan would like to write a story about us and how Doctor Chung saw you in my future. She thinks it would help others learn about Doctor Chung and his fantastic talent. I do want you to meet the doctor, Leonard, darling. He is truly a wonderful man."

"Sure, I'd be happy to. You're a writer, too?" Leonard directed the question at me. I continued to get the impression I made him nervous.

Gladys answered for me. "He is Susan's research assistant."

Susan took advantage of the moment to ask him, "I'd like to interview you for the story."

"Me? What? I don't know anything about this doctor."

Gladys jumped to Leonard's defense. "Leonard is a very private person, aren't you, darling?"

"Yes, private. I like to keep my business to myself."

"Maybe just a few facts?" Susan put on her best smile. "The story is not only about the doctor. It's about you and Gladys as well. Nothing too intrusive. Say, your profession. A few details of your personal history. I'd like to flesh you out as the person who has made such a profound effect on Gladys."

"I'll have to think about it," Leonard said, sliding his hand onto the crook of Glady's elbow. "Shall we go to your place, honey?"

Gladys addressed Susan. "Leonard and I will talk things over, but the story you're looking into involves really only me and Doctor Chung. He saw Leonard in my future. Maybe you should interview Doctor Chung rather than Leonard." She offered Leonard a supportive grin, and he said softly, "Thank you."

"We'll be in touch," Gladys said over her shoulder, and she and Leonard headed east until Leonard waved down a cab.

"What do you think?" Susan asked, tapping on her phone. "I have to get back to the office."

"I can take the train. I don't know. He doesn't seem to be very well preserved."

"I know. He needed a shave."

"And his shoes were scuffed."

"We have his name."

"If it is his name."

Susan laughed. "The private eye in you is leaking out."

I shrugged. "Okay, we'll research Leonard Faraday and see what shows up."

Susan leaned in and pecked my cheek as her Uber approached. "Talk to you soon."

I helped her into the car and slammed the back door. Then I headed off to the A train.

Twenty

"He wasn't any..." I thought for a moment. "...Clark Gable." I wanted to put my description of Leonard Faraday into terms Henny would understand.

"Cary Grant, maybe?"

"Definitely not. No, none of those guys. Not a great face. Not much hair. Oh, and scuffed shoes and a five o'clock shadow."

"Sound like she's salvaging him, not falling in love with him."

"She's no prize either," I commented. "Seems to be well off, though."

"Ah, now you're making sense. What's Susan think?"

"Same as me. Something's weird. Why don't you call Thursday? Ask about the doctor and see if he knows anything about a Leonard Faraday. Be sure you tell him no turtles are involved in this case."

Henny smiled. "Can't hurt, I guess." He made the call but didn't bother to put it on speaker, so I made myself a cup of coffee and waited for a report. I wondered whether it made sense for Henny and me to pay Doctor Chung a visit. Under what guise could we pop in on him, though? Plus, it wouldn't be wise to interfere with Susan's story unless she okayed it. Getting involved more deeply right now sounded too complicated, so I sipped my coffee but didn't stop mulling over the good doctor. For one thing, I'd like to get a look at this man who could see the future. Maybe I could go as a paying customer, but then I recalled his five-hundred-dollar fee.

Too bad we didn't have a client who'd foot the bill for me. Henny ended his call.

"So, what did Thursday say?"

"He knows about Chung. He's who put Susan onto him. No crimes committed, though. Naturally, the name Leonard Faraday didn't ring a bell, but he said he'd check and get back to me."

The afternoon slipped by with me keeping Archie Goodwin company as he did the leg work around New York City for Nero Wolfe and Henny fussing, as usual, with his toothpicks. As we wrapped things up for the day and Henny stood in front of our wall mirror adjusting his fedora, I asked whether he wanted to have a drink in Giandos on the way home, my treat. He agreed. We never got there, though.

As we were walking out of the office, my cell chimed.

"Susan," I mouthed to Henny. She spoke quickly and told me where to meet her.

I pocketed my phone and stared at Henny.

"What?" he asked, frowning.

"A friend of Gladys Rutherford found her dead on the living room floor of her apartment about forty minutes ago. Face black and blue, likely strangled."

"Jeez. Was the boyfriend there?"

"Susan said no."

"Interesting."

"Isn't it."

~ * ~

When Henny and I arrived in front of Gladys Rutherford's building, we encountered Susan pacing the sidewalk. Yellow tape blocked most of the apartment building's doorway, and police allowed no one in without first inspecting their IDs.

"They won't let me in," Susan complained.

"But you're sure the old lady is dead?" Henny asked.

"I'm sure. I did manage a minute with a detective I recognized."

"Did you get a chance to tell him you just had lunch with Gladys?"

"No, he was understandably in a hurry. I think you should call Detective Thursday, Henny." Henny conducted most of our communications with him. "Tell him what we know and tell him we're catching pneumonia standing outside."

Henny took out his cell phone and stepped away.

"How'd you find out about her?" I asked Susan. We both turned our backs to the chilly wind whipping between the buildings.

"I was in the office and heard the buzz go around. Somebody's always monitoring police emergencies."

"You said somebody went to visit Gladys and found her?"

"I got that from the detective I spoke with."

"Who opened the apartment door for this friend?"

Susan shook her head. "I don't know, but I think the friend's still up there."

I glanced at Henny who was talking away on his phone. "And no sign of the boyfriend we met?"

"I don't think so. I'd really like to go up to the apartment and talk to some people."

Henny rejoined us. "Thursday thanks us for the tip. He's making some calls."

"Meaning?" Susan asked.

"He'll try to get us access to the crime scene."

I could see Henny perk up when he said, "access to the crime scene." I don't know whether the expression came from a *noir* forties' novel in Henny's collection or a sixties' detective TV series, but he definitely got a thrill using it.

No more than seven or eight minutes passed before Susan's eyes widened.

"Here comes the detective I mentioned."

"Good, you're still here," the man said by way of greeting. He was tall and thin, wearing only a blue sport coat to keep warm. "Would you like to come upstairs? It's too cold for you to be standing out like this."

Susan followed the detective, and Henny and I followed Susan, hoping we were included in the detective's concern about the lack of warmth. Without a hitch, he led us to the elevator and the sixth floor. Technicians and a couple medical people stood about, finished, I supposed, with what they came to do. A body covered by a sheet lay on a wheeled stretcher, ready to be transported wherever protocol demanded. As we watched the stretcher roll out the door, two men in blue escorted a woman from a bedroom. The woman collapsed onto the sofa and buried her face in her hands, snuffling in sadness. She was short, not much overweight, wore a flowered dress, and appeared to be in Gladys Rutherford's age group. Her short brown hair was minimally streaked with gray.

The detective who'd escorted us took us aside.

"I'm Detective Moore. I got a call from Detective Thursday. He said you have some information about what went on... what might have gone on... here."

Susan introduced us and took the lead in relating the details of our luncheon with Gladys, as well as the events leading up to the meal.

"Leonard Faraday. Thursday's already put out an alert for him. We'll pick him up eventually. Do you think this weird Doctor Chung figures in this somewhere?"

"Hard to say," Susan answered.

Henny added, "Looks like he couldn't see Gladys's future as clearly as he thought."

"We'd better question him, I suppose," Moore said.

The woman on the sofa had ceased snuffling, so Detective Moore sat and spoke with her. She recounted paying a random visit to her friend and finding the apartment door ajar and the woman stretched out on the floor. No one else was in the apartment, she assured us, and as soon as she'd gathered her wits, she called 911. That's all she knew. She'd never met Leonard Faraday, though Gladys had mentioned him to her in a phone call. Gladys had recommended that she—her name was June Mayall, and she lived three floors below the deceased—pay a visit to Doctor Chung, who was an amazing man and that she, Gladys, would tell her everything about him when they next met. The distraught woman began to snuffle again, so we left her in peace.

Susan had an intent look in her eye as we descended to the lobby. When the elevator door opened, she remained inside the car.

"I'm going back up... no, wait." She stepped out of the car. "Let me call Doctor Chung. I'll tell him I'm sending over my two best researchers. He seemed to perk up when I told him I worked for the *Post*. Stay there." Susan took a few steps away and made her call.

"What are we researching?" I asked.

Henny shrugged. "Whatever Susan tells us to. Don't frown. Here she comes." He gestured toward Susan, stepping toward us.

"He'll see you, but you have to leave by four-forty-five. He's meeting a client at five. I didn't mention anything about Gladys. You tell him and get his initial reaction. Do you have the card I gave you?"

Henny pulled it from his pocket.

"Okay," Susan said. "I'm going back up."

Henny stopped her.

"Wait. Do you still have the book we gave you? The old Doctor Chung book?"

Susan dug into her pocket. "Yeah, here. Good thinking. It might come in handy. I'll talk to you tonight." The final sentence she directed at me before the elevator doors closed on her.

I looked at Henny. "I repeat, what are we researching?"

"What if... what if Chung already knows about Gladys lying on the living room floor?"

"How could he? Unless..."

"Right. Unless. When we spring the news to him, we need to gauge his reaction closely. *Real* closely." Henny checked his watch. "We don't have a lot of time. Let's take a cab and discuss our approach on the way."

Twenty-one

Nothing more than a wooden sign hung in the long window of the door to Doctor Chung's storefront. Dark, wrinkled curtains hung behind the door and over the large window to its left. Not much curb appeal, but perhaps appropriate to the doctor's profession. Metal letters attached to the sign said only *Doctor So Yen Chung*. And beneath the name, *Transcendentalist*. To the left stood an herb store and to the right a store specializing in *Vinyl Records: Old and New*. I suggested to Henny he might want to pick up some Glenn Miller on the way out.

"I already have six different copies of "In the Mood." Do I need seven? Anyway, not much of his I don't already have," Henny spat out one toothpick and inserted another. "Come on. He's waiting for us. It's way after four."

We crossed the street and entered the unlocked door. The aroma of incense met us head on. The lights were dim and tinged red. The opening of the door must have sent a signal into the rear—

or perhaps Doctor Chung simply sensed our arrival—because a slight Asian man wearing loose pants and a thin jacket of Eastern design stepped out from behind a white curtain, pink in the light, and approached us. He had wisps of hair across his scalp and a thin mustache.

"Are you Doctor Chung?" I asked.

"Yes, I am," he answered in a soft voice.

"I believe you're expecting us. Susan Denzler phoned you. He's Henny, and I'm Lloyd, Ms. Denzler's co-workers."

"Yes, please join me in back." He held the curtain aside, and we entered a small room having a square table, nothing more than a card table most likely, covered with a draping white cloth and a few folding metal chairs. Against the wall was a smaller table covered with tea-making gear. The reddish lights remained on the other side of the curtain.

"Sit, please," the doctor said. "I can offer you some tea."

The doctor positioned three chairs around the table. The light from the ceiling panels didn't exceed forty watts. The tea was already brewed, and two tiny cups were in front of Henny and me right away. I knew enough from my trips to Chinatown to identify the aroma of jasmine tea.

"Now, gentleman, how can I help you? Ms. Denzler has been kind enough to offer me some notice in her newspaper."

"And that has helped your business?" I asked.

Doctor Chung bowed his head and smiled.

"I don't mean at all to be rude," I said, "but what exactly is your business? I admit the word transcendentalism doesn't mean much to me."

"Yes. I am able in many cases to entwine my spirit with the spirit of another. With the gift I've been given and with sufficient concentration, the life of that person, past and future, reveals itself to me."

"I see." I looked at Henny, who took over for the moment.

Henny asked, "Do you communicate with those who have passed away?"

Chung smiled indulgently. "You are having fun with me? I do not claim any such ability. Such... such... no, it would... what is the word... triv... ...make small what I do."

"Trivialize," Henny prompted.

"Yes, trivialize," Chung agreed.

"Doctor Chung, did you learn this gift from your grandfather? Has it been passed through the generations?"

A small twitch of a muscle above his nose indicated he was not used to being challenged to explain his capabilities.

"My ability grew in me from my childhood."

That didn't quite answer Henny's question, so I asked, "But you must have been taught by your grandfather. I'm assuming your grandfather wrote the famous book. Or was it your father?"

Henny took the book out and put it on the table. "We've read the book. It's fascinating. Do you know how your...?"

Chung stared at the book for a moment. "Yes, that is my grandfather's book. It is very rare."

He stared at us as if awaiting an explanation, but Henny merely finished his question. "Do you know how your grandfather acquired his talent? Did his grandfather have the same talent? Was his ability the same as yours?"

Doctor Chung adjusted himself in his chair and took a sip of tea.

"Our family, yes, has been blessed for generations. It appears to come to us naturally. It is our family inheritance, our heritage. It is unwise to question the wonderous workings of, shall we call it, nature?"

"Sure," Henny agreed. "Let's call it nature. You seem, however, not to have put your ability to use until recently. Why is that?"

Henny had hit upon a powerful question. Doctor Chung was not an old man nor was he very young. Mid-forties is the youngest he could have been. Why only now was he making a splash with his knowledge of the future?

"I am new to this country."

"Where were you before you arrived in New York?" Henny asked.

Chung took another sip of tea. "In the East. China, Nepal, Tibet. There are many things to learn."

"So, your ability... you must study to perfect it?"

"One must always study. Like a glorious golden statue, my special talent must be polished and cherished to bring it to its brightest... what is the word...lusper?"

"Luster," Henny corrected.

Chung dipped his head and accepted the revision gracefully.

"I must prepare for a new believer. She will be here soon," Chung reminded us. I checked my watch. Twenty-five minutes until five. I wanted to get Gladys into the conversation.

"Doctor, you've been working with a woman by the name of Gladys Rutherford."

"Yes, a fine woman with a bright future."

"And you gave her much hope about her future."

"Yes, companionship, even love. Yes. She will be happy."

"Well, I don't think so," I said.

Chung tilted his head in puzzlement. "What do you mean?" The little muscle above the doctor's nose jumped again.

"I'm afraid she's met with an accident. Did you sense she was in any danger?"

Henny took the book back and folded his arms.

"Danger? No."

"She's been murdered," I announced. "We've come here directly from her apartment and can tell you so for a fact."

"Dead? Murdered? I don't... How... Are you certain?"

"As I said, we were there and saw the situation."

"How can it be? This is shocking. I have someone coming... I must compose myself. Please." He rose and really seemed thrown by the news. "Please," he repeated and gestured toward the curtain. "I don't see how..."

Henny and I rose and let ourselves into the other room. Doctor Chung stood holding the curtain, backlit by the smaller room.

"We're sorry to have sprung such news on you so abruptly," I said.

"Please, I must prepare," Chung replied.

Henny and I let ourselves out onto MacDougal Street and shut the door behind us.

"Over there," Henny said, gesturing.

We crossed the street and stood in a vacant doorway.

Henny let out a sigh. "I don't think he knew."

I agreed. "I don't think he did either. He sure acted like it was news to him."

"You think he studied in Nepal and those other places?"

"*Pssshh!* He can no more see into the future than I can. He'd be investing in the stock market if he could. That's what I'd do."

Henny grunted in agreement. "Now what?"

"Why don't we do what Susan did?"

"Which was?"

"See who goes in for his five o'clock session and wait for her... he said her, right?"

"Yeah."

"Wait for her to come out and see if she'll talk to us." I pointed down the street to the right. "There's a coffee shop we can take her to if need be."

A few minutes before five, I spotted a woman who did not look much like a Greenwich Village type. Wrapped in fur with a scarf tied under her chin, she examined the address numbers on the stores she passed. I tapped Henny and pointed. When she reached Doctor's Chung's door, she paused and walked slowly past, then turned back and stood before the door, seeming to stare at the window sign. Her hand reached for the knob, but she drew it back. I thought for a moment she might abandon her desire to peek into the future, but finally, she grasped the doorknob and entered the eerie room.

"Nothing to do but wait," Henny mumbled.

We didn't have to wait long, less than ten minutes, before the woman reappeared. I glimpsed Chung as he closed the door behind her. She stood motionless on the sidewalk, and before she could decide what course to take, Henny and I were with her. Henny took the lead.

"Excuse me, ma'am. I see you've been in to see Doctor Chung. He's really marvelous, isn't he?"

"*Humph*, not today he wasn't. He was abrupt and rude." She caught herself before going further. She glared at the two of us. "Who are you? Have you been to see Doctor Chung?"

"We were in with him just before you arrived," Henny admitted. "Can we talk to you about him?"

"What do you know about him?" the woman asked, an edge to her voice.

"We know what he told us." Henny produced the book. "We're looking into him. It seems his grandfather also was gifted. This book was written by his grandfather over seventy-five years ago." The woman took the book and glanced at the title page.

"Same name," she said, meeting Henny's gaze.

I added, "To be honest, we do know a few other things about him." I produced the ten-dollar tin detective badge I'd bought in a Times Square souvenir shop which had come in handy more than once. "Can we buy you coffee and talk? There's a shop a few doors down. We may be helping you."

I returned the badge to my pocket, and she returned the book to Henny.

"I think I *would* like to hear what you have to tell me," she decided. A few minutes later, we were seated at a table in the coffee shop.

Twenty-two

I formally introduced Henny and me, and the woman introduce herself as Miriam Rappaport.

"I can't imagine what was wrong with Doctor Chung today," she said after we'd ordered coffee and a few buns to nibble on. "Was he like that when you saw him?"

Henny gave me a surreptitious nod. "We'll get into that," I promised. "Had you visited the doctor before?"

"Yes, a week ago. He told me to come back this week, today, but he practically threw me out of his rooms. We had no session whatsoever. He wants me back in another week."

"What went on in your first visit with him?"

"Well, sitting here like this with you two gentlemen...I feel somewhat foolish."

"By no means," I assured her. "We've been looking into the doctor for a while."

"'Looking into?' What does that mean?"

"We are dubious he has the skill he claims to have. It's likely a..." I edited out the word scam. "...put on."

Miriam was having trouble making eye contact with me. She looked about the same age as Gladys Rutherford and seemed to be from the same social set. Her hair was dyed an attractive blond, not inappropriate to her face and figure. She'd held up well.

I continued. "Can you tell us why you went to see Doctor Chung?"

Miriam sighed and at last gave me a steady gaze. "A friend of mine visited him and proclaimed him a wonder. And the future he foretold for her, came true."

Henny spoke. "Did he foresee romance entering her life?" The question stunned Miriam. She ran her tongue across her lips and swallowed before answering. "Yes. She met a man soon after, *very* soon after, as the doctor assured her she would."

My stomach did a little jig, but I managed to ask the question. "And the doctor told you last week that he needed to experience your spirit for seven days before his vision unfolded your future. In fact, he held your hand for much of last week's session to experience your... being."

A crevice formed between Miriam's eyes. She made as if to speak but stayed silent.

"Miriam, may I call you Miriam?" I asked.

"Of course. What were you going to say?"

"It's possible this is merely a routine Chung goes through with any woman who walks through his door."

"Mr. Lloyd, I am not a stupid woman."

"I didn't mean to suggest that you were."

She shook her head. "Are you telling me he's done this before? It's a show he puts on?"

"He has done it before."

"Often?"

"We can only swear to one other time, but that one time is why we're looking into him."

"You think he's a con artist?"

"What do you think?" Henny interjected.

"I'm feeling very foolish right now. But what he told Gladys came true. I know it did. She told me about it."

Henny and I shared a glance, and he asked the question. "Would that be Gladys Rutherford of East Thirty-Seventh Street near First Avenue?"

Miriam's mouth dropped open, and she stared at Henny. "How... how do you know...? What is going on here?"

I reached across and covered Miriam's hand with my own.

"We have some very bad news for you. I'm afraid your friend Gladys is dead."

"Dead! I just spoke to her yesterday."

"Nonetheless, she was murdered this afternoon."

"Murdered?" Had Miriam been on her feet, she would have collapsed. As it was, she slumped back in her chair, clasping her hands across her chest.

"This is a nightmare. You don't think... not the doctor. What... what...?"

I raised a hand to quiet Miriam. "Take some breaths. I'll tell you what we know." I went through Glady's experience with Chung, then told Miriam about our luncheon that day and about Gladys's going off afterward with Leonard. "We visited Doctor Chung today to inform him of Glady's death. You saw the results when you went in for your session."

"I certainly did. Yes," Miriam said softly. "Leonard was the name she mentioned."

"Another friend, June Mayall, found Gladys's apartment door open and her on the floor. The boyfriend was nowhere in sight."

"June, yes. I know June. We're good friends. We three live in the same building. June planned to pay a visit to Doctor Chung, too. My god, this is awful. The police must be looking for the boyfriend?"

"Yes," Henny assured her.

"What should I do?" Miriam said, looking first at Henny, then at me.

I answered, "The only thing you can do is go home, and I would suggest staying away from Doctor Chung, at least until the boyfriend is arrested and it's proven Doctor Chung is merely a coincidence in all of this."

"Yes, yes. I don't need romance in my life badly enough to... well, you understand."

"We do," Henny said. "Can we take you home?"

"I can't believe Gladys is gone. She lived three floors below me. Yesterday, we were on the phone together."

"You can call the building, if you'd like," Henny suggested.

"I think not. I believe you, but it's so... unbelievable."

Miriam's oxymoron aside, we saw her to the street. She declined our offer to accompany her home, and Henny waved down a cab for her.

"Will you keep in touch with me and let me know what's happening?" Miriam asked. She opened her purse and pulled out a card. On it were her name and phone number.

I pocketed the card and promised to let her know the moment something broke.

Henny closed the cab door, and Miriam went home.

Henny and I voted unanimously not to return to the office but instead headed to Giandos in our own cab. On the way, I called Susan, who reminded me she had a banquet to attend at eight o'clock that night, along with other *New York Post* stalwarts, but with her *Post* Uber account in hand there'd be time for her to make a stop at Giandos so we could hash over the mysterious Doctor Chung for a while.

"I love hearing you say that," Henny complimented. "'The Mysterious Doctor Chung.'"

"Very *noir*, eh?" I said, smiling. "I kind of like saying it myself."

~ * ~

We settled in at the bar and soon Roderigo had glasses of wine in front of us. "What do we make of things?" I asked.

"Chung was shaken by Gladys's murder. Agreed? In front of us and in front of Miriam Rappaport."

"Agreed. And not simply because he had a passing business acquaintance with her. Something more. Agreed?"

Henny nodded slowly. "Yeah. And he's got a pattern. Older lady with money. Pay a visit. Wait a week."

"We're sort of in the rough there, don't you think?"

"The rough?"

I frowned. "A golf metaphor. Out of bounds a bit. Do two women make a pattern?"

"Sure. Can't you see how Chung worked his way up to these women? Got himself a reputation with the earlier stunts."

"Stunts?"

"The incidents Susan told us about. Easily staged. Throw a wallet with twenty bucks where somebody could find it. Mail two baseball tickets to a guy. Give out business cards. Somehow his behavior made its way to Detective Thursday, to the *Post* and to Susan and eventually to Gladys, who spilled the news to her two friends."

"Why kill Gladys, though? It's sure to spook the other women."

"Obviously not part of the plan."

"And the plan was..."

"Money, what else. Get money."

"Awfully roundabout way and a murder is a crazy deviation from any sensible plan."

Henny shrugged. "That's what I said."

"Chung can't be doing this alone," I went on.

"No, no. You're right. Leonard...?"

"Part of the... the gang."

"There must be others. Maybe Chung's running a marriage bureau. He finds rich women for destitute men."

"The women may be looking for husbands, but I doubt the men are looking for wives. Probably nothing more than trying to squeeze as much money out of these women as possible. Maybe from figuring out how to rob them, or maybe depending on the stars in the lady's eyes and her misplaced generosity."

"Maybe Gladys was a robbery gone bad." Henny shrugged again. "Who knows?"

"And why are we so interested? We don't have a client. We're not getting paid. Bank accounts tend to wither when you don't get paid and have bills coming due."

"Sam Spade couldn't have said it better. Another?"

Henny got Roderigo's attention and a second glass of wine arrived. Two sips into the second wine, Susan walked in dressed for her banquet, and boy, did she look good. It struck me that I had never really taken Susan any place special enough that would encourage her to dress up the way she did tonight in a spaghetti-strapped, tight, spangly dress which showed off her lovely legs. Makeup in places I didn't usually notice makeup. And she smelled good.

"You didn't look like this the last time I saw you," I said, kissing her and enjoying her aroma.

"Approve?" she asked, doing a pirouette.

"Very much so," I said.

"Me too," Henny chimed in.

"I had to bolt from the crime scene and didn't have much time to do my hair. How's it look?"

"You look great all around," I said.

Susan took a seat and ordered a pinot grigio from Roderigo. "So, what's up?"

I went over Henny's and my trip to Chung's office, his getting unhinged on hearing the news of the murder, and our meeting with the quickly dismissed Miriam Rappaport. I included Henny's and my bar-thoughts while we waited for her on the ins and outs of the Chung case. Susan listened, nodding a few times.

"You two are absolutely right. Something is rotten in the state of Greenwich Village."

"That's from *Hamlet*, sort of," I instructed Henny.

"I know that," he snapped.

"Don't get touchy. We don't have a client, Susan."

"So, this case is a blemish on your income?" Susan offered, raising her eyebrows.

"We need income," I argued.

"Let me see the card today's woman gave you. She said she was a friend of Gladys?"

"Yeah, and with the other woman, too. June Mayall."

"Maybe I can put the two of them together to hire you to keep them out of trouble. It would give them something to talk about with others in their circle."

"Sounds good to me," I said.

"But that's a job for tomorrow. I'm off to the Hilton near Radio City. The *Post* is getting an award. Sports section. And a free, fancy dinner. Win, win." She flicked her empty wineglass with her finger and rose from her chair. "Your treat?" she asked, smiling at me.

"Of course." I pecked her cheek and she left. Henny and I had a third wine and then went home for inexpensive apartment dinners.

Twenty-three

"He says he can't do it," Henny assured me next morning in the office.

"Why the heck not? Doesn't he want to crack the case?" The night before I'd gotten an idea—one of Henny's 'insights.' If Chung were running a scam, he couldn't be doing it alone. We'd pretty much established that the night before over wine in Giandos. So, he had a gang. I'd used the word 'gang' again because I knew Henny liked the atmosphere it created. What we needed to do was have Detective Thursday stake out Chung's place and follow or question any man or men who showed up and looked like part of the gang. My idea hadn't left the runway, though.

"He says there's no real link between Gladys lying dead on the floor and Chung the Transcendentalist. Plus, he can't spare the manpower."

"Leonard doesn't count as a link?"

"No."

"You described Chung's reaction when we told him about Gladys?"

"I did. He didn't make much of it. He did say to call him if we developed anything concrete."

Thursday's reaction ticked me off. "He's got thousands of officers at his beck and call. Why doesn't *he* develop something concrete?"

"You know they're working on the Gladys end. There is no Chung end yet, except for me and you."

I got out of my desk chair to pace. I walked to the bank of windows and stared for a moment down at frigid Centre Street.

"We don't have a client, remember?" Henny reminded me. "Let's find a crime with a client... *something* with a client."

My cell made its noise, so I went back to my desk and took the call. It was Susan, excitedly informing me that Miriam and June wanted to meet with Henny and me at noon in Miriam's apartment. They were thinking of hiring us to get to the bottom of Doctor Chung.

~ * ~

Noon found Henny and me at Miriam Rappaport's apartment three floors above where Gladys was slain. June Mayall was there, too, sitting on the sofa, hands in her lap, a countenance as stiff as a starched shirt.

"Thanks for coming so quickly," Miriam said, holding her apartment door open for us. Henny and I each found a chair, and Miriam joined her friend on the sofa.

June opened the discussion. "Tell us what you know about this Doctor Chung. The way Gladys raved about him made it seem like he was the greatest thing since sliced bread." She was much older than Henny and me but not old enough, I thought, to use a sliced bread comparison. As far as I knew, there had always been sliced bread. Henny, though, took the initiative and gave an honest account of our limited experiences with Doctor Chung and Gladys.

When he finished, June unfolded her hands and asked, "Did Doctor Chung kill our friend?"

"I'm certain he didn't," Henny answered.

"There, you see," she said to Miriam, adding a definitive bob of her head.

Henny added a caution. "He could, though, have been involved in some fashion. There's no hard evidence that he was yet, but you never know."

"There, now, see," Miriam said to June. To Henny, she said, "How was he involved?"

"I didn't say he *was* involved. But the storyline is suspicious, don't you agree? He predicts a new man in Gladys's life; a new man shows up. The new man pitches himself to your friend, who is open to such an approach—"

June interrupted. "Gladys was a very lonely woman. You know that as well as I, Miriam. You know how she used to go on over her husband's death. And she loved talking with any man who would talk back to her. I've even seen her flirting with the man who stocks the bananas in Whole Foods."

"Please," Miriam insisted, "let Mr. Henny finish. Go on."

"Well, as I was saying, Leonard finds her, and your friend is much taken by the fellow..."

"According to what you said, he wasn't much to look at," June said.

"Please!" Miriam scolded.

Her friend gave a stubborn shake of her head but allowed Henny to continue.

"Can we allow that no one, including Doctor Chung, can see into the future?"

Miriam looked down. June cleared her throat, stuck out her chin, and said, "Gladys believed he could, and wanted us to give him a chance to tell us whether he saw... men... romance... in our future. He wasn't wrong about Gladys's future, you know."

The women shared a glance, and Miriam said, "This is embarrassing."

"Embarrassing or not. We agreed to find out whether Doctor Chung is a phony and whether Gladys was right in believing in him and suggesting to us that we... we... use his services."

Miriam did not argue back. "Yes," she said, moving her gaze from Henny to me, then back to Henny. "We do want to know that."

Their interest in hiring us was becoming clear to me, so I asserted myself.

"Henny and I have already begun a preliminary investigation into the doctor as part of our relationship with Ms. Denzler, the reporter for the *Post*. We met Ms. Rappaport when she left the doctor's storefront."

"Call me Miriam, please."

"That's how we met Miriam. If you'd like to hire us to continue—"

"We do," June said, not letting me finish my sentence. "Right, Miriam? I have great confidence in these two gentlemen. They strike me as powerful people. Don't they you, Miriam?"

"Thank you, Ms. Mayall," I said, feeling impressed with myself over the impact we'd made.

"Call me, June, please."

Miriam's face had turned a slight pink over June's gushing opinion.

"How much will this cost us?" June asked. "We want this information but won't be made paupers in the process."

"Of course not," I said in my most soothing voice. "Henny, it shouldn't take more than a week's solid work."

"Right," Henny said. He hated talking money matters, so I knew he'd clam up. I quickly did the math.

"Since there are two of you, four thousand dollars for one week of our total attention. At the end of that week, we'll talk, either to give you the truth about the doctor or to explain as much as we've uncovered."

"Two thousand each," June muttered. "I'm good with that. Miriam?"

"Yes," she muttered casting her eyes anywhere but on one of us.

Henny, though, had his detective mind working.

"Suppose," he began in a thoughtful tone, "suppose we need you ladies for something. Suppose we ask you to meet with the doctor."

"But if he killed..." Miriam burst out.

"Lloyd and I will always be nearby. Besides, I assure you he, himself, did not harm your friend. But the question is, if we need you, will you be available?"

"Absolutely," June cried. "If Miriam won't, I will."

"I will. I will," Miriam agreed in an agitated voice, not wanting to be left out.

"I left my checkbook downstairs," June said. "Miriam, pay the gentlemen, and I'll bring you a check first thing."

Miriam wrote the check; Henny and I promised to work hard and we took a cab back to the office.

~ * ~

Before we could settle into a strategy discussion, though, Henny's cell rang. He took the call and right away his eyes opened wide, and he looked at me.

"Where did you say? Okay. We're on our way."

"We're on our way where?" I asked. "We just sat down."

"Thursday would like us to identify a body."

That sentence stopped me cold. Susan flashed through my mind, but it couldn't be.

"Whose?"

"Maybe Leonard, if we can confirm it is Leonard."

I gave a small sigh of relief. "Where?"

"An alley off Crosby Street."

"Not much of a street." Crosby Street ran for only a few blocks below Houston Street.

"Why's he think it's Leonard?"

"Our description of him. He said to tell you the scuffed shoes clinched it. Clinched it if we can identify him."

"No ID on him?"

"None."

I stood. "We can be there in fifteen minutes if we walk quick. Let me give Susan a heads-up. She'll want to be in on this if she's free."

Susan was free. The body did belong to Leonard, and he still needed a shave and, of course, still wore his scuffed, black shoes. Shot in the chest once at close range. Susan hung around, hoping for more to write about, but Henny and I went back to the office, picking up some Chinese takeout on the way. I could tell the murder upset Henny because he hung his fedora neatly on our coat rack and didn't try to toss a ringer from his desk.

We ate quietly, occasionally offering one another an idle thought on what had happened. After disposing of our lunch debris, we gave both June and Miriam a call to warn them further against Doctor Chung, adding there was no evidence he had anything to do with Leonard's demise, but better safe than sorry. Then we sat at our desks and developed a plan of attack, which pleased neither of us. We'd let Thursday and the NYPD deal with Gladys and Leonard. Henny and I would concentrate on Chung, as we were being paid to do. Henny and I would split duty and stake out Chung's place of business. If he were involved in this, he couldn't be acting as a committee of one. At least, that was Henny's and my conclusion. I would go first and determine whether Chung was in his place of business or elsewhere. I would either see him arrive and with whom or follow him if he left. I would take a photo of anyone who entered or left his premises. I had to take first watch because Henny needed to go home and get 'into disguise.' His words. Getting into disguise for Henny meant changing from his usual pinstriped, double-breasted suit and fedora into a jogging outfit or something similar. And he was right. He looked like two different people, depending on his wardrobe. I simply dressed down and pulled a baseball cap low over my eyes.

It was a Friday night, and things were lively on MacDougal Street when I got there. Café Wha?, down the block, the club where Bob Dylan got his start, had a long line to get in. A couple of people were circulating and handing out free tickets to different comedy clubs. The bars and restaurants were hopping, so my pacing about across from Chung's Transcendental center evoked no curiosity. I still hadn't seen him by eight o'clock, but the reddish light from inside his emporium had been visible the whole time, leaking through any uncovered bit of window to the street. No one entered or left, and I stifled my curiosity as to whether the front door was locked or unlocked. At eight-thirty, Henny texted me, and I reported all quiet and all well.

A little after ten, Chung's place snapped into darkness, and the man himself stepped outside and scanned the vicinity. He turned his back to me to lock up, then started walking toward Sixth Avenue. I tailed him from the opposite side of the street. The night was chilly, but Mother Nature hadn't overdone it. Without any appreciable breeze to rub the cold in my face, it felt almost pleasant.

Chung wore a long black topcoat and a fedora Henny might have commented on—pro or con, I wasn't sure. He looked nothing like the Asian mystic he purported to be, and he moved with a quick determination not apparent when he was in costume. Turning left from Sixth onto Canal Street, he dodged the Holland Tunnel traffic and proceeded to Broadway, then right one block to Lispenard Street and another right. Lispenard, a dark and narrow street, ran for only two blocks and had very little to recommend it. Chung made a beeline to a bar in the middle of the first block and disappeared inside. The bar had a bank of small, square windows next to the narrow entry door, and I walked slowly by, peering in. The windows were grimy, though, and I didn't see much except a few glowing lights and a crowded bar. I texted Henny my location, not suggesting he join me, but only to keep him in the loop. I pulled my Mets cap lower and went inside.

I wriggled into a spot at the end of the bar nearest the front door, and while I waited for the Heineken I ordered, I located Chung through the jostling customers, sitting at a table with two other men in a far corner of the bar. It wasn't a large space and with the crowd to hide me, I had no trouble keeping him in view.

The bartender plopped the green beer bottle down in front of me—no glass offered in a place like this—and whenever I wanted to poke my head out for a better look, I simply lifted the bottle in front of my face and peeked around it. Chung and the two men were having an animated talk, Chung frequently tapping the table with his fingers to emphasize something he said. The two men spent a lot of time nodding. Suddenly, the three men burst into silent laughter; silent to me but I noticed a couple people near them turn and look their way. Then Chung took a coin from his pocket and gave it a flip with his thumb. He caught it and smacked it down on the table, keeping it covered with his hand. One man pointed to the other and the second man smiled and spoke what looked like one word. Chung uncovered the coin and both men leaned in. The man who'd called the flip gave another laugh as the first man slumped back in his chair. Chung seemed to soothe the loser, who took his defeat in good grace. The loser went to throw some money on the table, but Chung stopped him and tapped his own chest. The drinks were on him.

The man whose evening was over rose and made his way by me and out the door. Chung and the remaining man continued their conversation long enough for me to have a second Heineken, and finally, they left together. I tossed fifteen dollars on the bar and followed them outside. They stood on the corner of Broadway and Lispenard and, after a final few minutes of conversation, they separated. I decided to follow the stranger, since there would be no danger of his recognizing me. He went downtown on Broadway and turned left onto Franklin Street, a slim thoroughfare with cars parked on both sides of the street, making it even narrower. A few turns took us to Baxter Street, where the man entered a six-story walk-up building next to a Vietnamese restaurant.

I texted Henny I was on my way home but got no reply. He'd assured me he'd go to bed early and be ready to start his tail first thing in the morning. My text said I didn't think it would be necessary and not to leave until we'd spoken. I was confident I'd figured Doctor Chung out.

Twenty-four

Susan called my plan "iffy." Henny preferred a plan more concise than what I'd outlined. I argued my point with the two of them over the weekend and... I can't say I won them over, but I didn't lose the argument either, since neither of them had an alternative.

Henny made a good point, though. My plan to dispose of Doctor Chung did stretch over maybe two weeks, possibly even longer, so the sooner I put things into motion, the better. Once I'd mentioned to Henny that my plan came as an "insight," he nodded and said he understood.

On Monday morning, I called Miriam and set up a meeting with her and June for that afternoon at one in her apartment. I went alone and explained to them what I had in mind. It took a little persuading but finally, at two o'clock, Miriam placed a call to Doctor Chung, who, in his soft, slow, and mellifluous voice claimed to have been on the verge of calling her. He apologized for their previous disrupted encounter, explaining that he'd received distressing news only a short time before.

June wanted to be the one to meet Chung, but I told her that since she hadn't even had one meeting yet with the transcendentalist, it would have to be Miriam. June, though, sat in on the call, mumbling the numerous, unsavory things she'd like to do to the doctor if she ever got her hands on him. I shushed her more than once. Miriam set up a new appointment for herself the next day at noon. That took care of the first step.

~ * ~

Henny and I were waiting in June's apartment for Miriam to return from her meeting with Chung the next day. When she arrived, her first words were, "You were right. I do have romance in my future. Something about a warm glow surrounding me. Happiness was approaching." She held up a hand. "Don't ask. Yes, I acted all teenage bubbly as you suggested. Let's see in what magical manner this dreamboat of mine appears." We discussed Miriam's plans for the week, and I made my guess as to where Chung would set up an encounter. Miriam was a member of the East Side Community Church, an organization which held an All-Are-Welcome recruitment Meet and Greet once a month in a school lunchroom on East Thirty-Third Street. This month's gathering would take place Thursday night, starting at seven. It would provide easy access to Miriam for anyone who wanted to meet her, and I felt certain that Doctor Chung used the week between the two meetings with his victims to research them as thoroughly as time would allow. I would attend the Meet and Greet also and give Miriam the high sign if I recognized the winner of the coin flip.

"Pawning us off with the flip of a coin," June steamed. "If I get my hands on him..."

Step two was set and step three, June's part, loomed tomorrow.

The next day, Wednesday, June gave Doctor Chung a call and asked for a first meeting. She offered him praise and begged for the same service he'd given her friends, who couldn't stop talking about him, and on and on. She agreed to pay his fee, now raised to seven-hundred-fifty dollars a session. The doctor accommodated her with a ten a.m. meeting on Friday.

Susan insisted on joining me at the East Side Community Church Thursday night Meet and Greet. Once Henny learned Susan was going, he wanted in, too. I couldn't see anything wrong with it, as long as we arrived separately and kept apart, and so, the next step was in motion.

~ * ~

The school's lunchroom had two tables of donated food and soft drinks set out—no alcohol, although my mind did have a *Boone's That's All* lurking in a welcome corner. That would be for later, though. To add a touch of intimacy, half of the overhead lights were on and half off. A lot of gray, metal folding chairs were spread around. Miriam, one of the organizers, was already in attendance when I entered a few minutes past seven, and five minutes after that, in walked the winner of the coin flip. He hung up his overcoat among a row of hangers, and I saw he was dressed nicely in a blue sweater and gray pants. From where I stood, I could not detect any scuffs on his dark shoes, nor did he need a shave.

He walked around the room, scanning the crowd of sixty or seventy people. He found Miriam, and three minutes later engaged her in conversation. I moseyed her way and gave her the prearranged high sign, a tug of my ear, to let her know the gentleman she was talking to was the one. Then I headed for the sandwich table, and as I took my first bite of a roast beef sandwich, I saw Henny arrive. He stood next to me in front of the sandwiches, and I let him know the two prospective lovers had met. He grabbed a ham and cheese on rye and drifted to the other side of the room. Susan bustled in about seven-twenty, and after I clued her in, she wandered away.

I avoided the proselytizers from the East Side Community Church and at eight-thirty, Miriam and the coin-flipper got their coats and headed out, leaving the other true believers to clean up.

During our planning, Miriam had insisted one of us follow her home, and Henny had volunteered for the duty, so Susan and I took an Uber across town to Bocca di Bacco for drinks, and I had the distinct pleasure of listening to Susan praise me for my insight into Doctor Chung. A nice evening all around.

Henny reported to me later that night when he got home. Miriam and—the gentleman's name was Clarence—Clarence had a drink on Second Avenue, after which Clarence walked Miriam to her building. They planned to have dinner on Saturday, and, according to Miriam, Clarence had acted the perfect gentleman. In fact, she kind of liked him but assured Henny it was merely a passing fancy.

On Friday, June had her first meeting with Chung, and it went as we told her it would. Handholding, cosmic attuning, and a promise of a follow-up meeting in a week. According to June, she had ample opportunities to brain Chung with one of a pair of heavy metal Eastern statuettes, but she kept her cool. The following Wednesday, June called Chung and asked whether they could have their second meeting in her apartment, and Chung said they could. Friday at two p.m.

Miriam had dinner with Clarence not only on Saturday, but on Tuesday, Wednesday, and Thursday nights as well. She invited him to her apartment on Friday at one-thirty for lunch, and he accepted. The plan had lined up perfectly. My ducks were in a row and due to settle down on the lake thirty minutes apart.

~ * ~

I had trouble sleeping Thursday night, the next day being the day Chung's world would come tumbling down, according to my plan. What worried me was how smoothly things had gone so far. In my experience, it wasn't like the universe to be so accommodating, but I managed to get through the Friday morning without a nervous breakdown.

I arrived at Miriam's and June's apartment building about one-fifteen but didn't go in. I waited outside until I saw Clarence precede me into the lobby. He didn't know it, but Henny, Susan, Detective Thursday and two uniforms were lurking in Miriam's bedroom, a place he would never get to see. I went up to June's apartment, and she and I went over her assignment again. I'd be in her bedroom while she and Doctor Chung had their session, where he'd tell her that romance loomed in her future, after she handed over another seven-hundred-fifty bucks.

Then, at the first opportunity, she would... June's wall phone, which connected only to the front desk, rang. She picked up, listened a moment, then said, "Send him up." To me she said, "The doorman. Doctor Chung is here."

"Ten minutes early. Okay, okay. No problem. You know what to do. Any questions?"

"None."

I disappeared into the bedroom, leaving the door ajar so I could hear. Showtime, I told myself.

I heard the apartment door open and close, then the low buzz of two people greeting one another. I noticed a skimpy, lace nightgown tossed across the bottom of June's bed, but I quickly dismissed it from my consciousness.

June asked for Chung's coat, then offered him tea. Chung declined and began his mumbo jumbo.

"Reach out your hands to me. Yes, by all means, move your chair closer."

Twenty seconds of quiet followed. Then Chung began a slow as molasses oration in his flutey voice about what he could see and what he could feel when he held June's hands and absorbed her emanations. He'd been concentrating, he said, on her since their first meeting, and there was a radiant, positive glow about her. She had nothing to fear. Happiness surrounded her. Fresh beginnings were imminent. A new person would soon make a profound difference in her life. Her remaining open to positive experiences in her coming days was crucial. He had a dozen more platitudes at his beck and call and used them to weave his web expertly about June. My phone gave a silent vibration. Henny, texting, "All well?" I texted back, "Yes, he's here."

June's voice took over from Chung. "I know what you mean," she said in the same kind of floating-in-air tone Chung used. "I have a special feeling. I see you. I see what approaches for you."

What was she jabbering about? All she needed to do was to keep Chung active until one-fifty. She had no business mimicking Chung's mumbo jumbo. There was no need to predict Chung's future, which I hoped would play out very nicely in the next few minutes.

"I can feel what's ahead for you," she continued. "A change is coming. A relocation. Have you been considering going away? No, do not release my hands. Don't break our rapport."

Their rapport? Threaten him with going away? What the devil was she doing? If she bollixed up my plan at the last moment... I felt like rushing out and giving her a slap.

"There, yes," June went on. "Oh, oh. The vision has faded. You may release me now. I feel so wonderful. I know your future will be satisfying to many people."

"You seem to have a talent yourself, Ms. Mayall," came Chung's voice.

"No, please, you must stay a while longer. I have a friend who wants to use your services. In fact, there are a number of friends I've told about you. They want to see you and speak to you. Since you're here now, why not meet one who is nearby?"

"Well, I..."

"She and my other friends know your abilities and their obligations to you. Your fee won't be any problem. They want to meet you so badly."

I breathed a little easier. June seemed back on track.

"Come with me. I can take you to my best friend and one by one, you can service the others. I know my friend will recommend you to them as highly as I have done."

"You're very kind, Ms. Mayall. I do have some time right now."

"Wonderful! Please, come with me."

I noticed my heart pumping and breathed slowly until I heard the apartment door open and close. They were on their way to Miriam's apartment, and I texted Henny. I went to the door, and through the security eyehole, peeked out into the empty hallway. Then I took the stairs six flights to the ninth floor. I stood in the stairwell catching my breath and waiting for Henny's all clear text, picturing what was going on inside Miriam's apartment. She and Clarence would be sitting at a table finishing up lunch. Miriam would have made certain the apartment door was unlocked. June would lead Doctor Chung unannounced into the apartment where Clarence would likely turn and see him, and Chung's mouth would drop open to see Clarence. Henny, Thursday, the two uniforms, and Susan would pop out of the bedroom. Henny would text me when it was safe to enter... and there it was; Henny's text!

I hustled to the apartment and went in to practically the identical tableau I'd imagined. Chung and Clarence, one sitting and one standing, stared at one another aghast. The uniforms had surrounded the two men as much as two people could perform a surrounding maneuver. And June was rambling on.

"Who exactly did you think you were, *Doctor* Chung? You're no more a doctor than I am. See how I foretold your future? You *are* going away. Do you believe me now? Tell us; tell us immediately. What happened to Gladys? What happened to Leonard, the man you sicced on her?"

Detective Thursday waved a hand at Henny, who did his best to move June off center stage and quiet her.

"You two know one another, it seems," Thursday said. To Chung, he said, "Where do you find these men?"

"Men? Men? What men?" Chung asked, looking left, right, and center for a sympathetic face.

"Where did he find you, pal? Clarence, isn't it?" Thursday asked.

"Find? Me?" Clarence looked left, right, and center for a sympathetic face, but had no better luck in finding one than Chung had.

"Which one of you owns a gun?" Thursday asked. "I have two search warrants waiting. One for your set up, Chung, and one for your apartment, Clarence."

"I don't own a gun," Clarence cried. "No, no. I'm just... he hired me. I have no gun."

"You own a gun, Chung? We'll find it if you do."

Chung stood mute.

Thursday said, "Take them downtown. We'll get the story out of them. I'll give the go-ahead for the searches."

Thursday stepped away to make a cell call, and the two uniforms handcuffed Chung and Clarence and took them away.

"I'm going with them," Susan said. "I'll be in touch." She reached out and slid her palm across my cheek. "Good job," she said, adding the prettiest smile I'd ever seen, considering the circumstances.

A moment later, Miriam, June, Henny, and I were left by ourselves.

"Well," I said, "that went well, I think." June bustled my way and put her arms around me.

"You were wonderful," she gushed, crushing her cheek to my chest.

Miriam, though, took her to task. "June, please. These are professional men."

June gave me one last squeeze and stepped back. "And why can't professional men be wonderful?"

"No reason," Miriam snapped. "But please, have some decorum. Tell him what we've decided if you want to make him feel wonderful."

June smiled my way, but this time included Henny in her happiness. "Miriam and I decided that if things went well, and you managed to get this faker Chung out of circulation, we would double your fee. After all, it took longer than the original week we paid you for. It was my idea, but Miriam agreed right away." June had thrown up one hand and spoken the second clause of her final sentence quickly to prevent Miriam from mentioning her decorum again. Miriam simply sighed and shook her head.

June went to a small table and took out a checkbook. "You can give me back later, Miriam." June wrote the check and handed it over. "Feel free to visit at any time."

"Thank you very much," Henny replied as I pocketed the check. "Lloyd, back to the office?"

"You bet," I agreed. We'd finished with Chung's mumbo jumbo, but now June was giving me the heebie-jeebies. "You must realize, though, it will be up to the officials involved—police, courts and such, to make certain Chung is no longer a Doctor of Transcendentalism."

"Miriam and I are prepared to testify against him," June assured us. "Aren't we, Miriam."

"Indeed, we are. We thank you both."

Henny and I nodded our 'your welcomes' and beat a path back to the office.

Twenty-five

I stopped at our Citibank branch on the way back to Centre Street and deposited June's check, and, surprisingly, Henny and I had the decency to wait until six o'clock before we broke out the *Boone's That's All*. Susan called about six-thirty, as I was topping off our glasses, and reported that Clarence had described Chung's scheme as far as it concerned him, and it did, naturally, involve taking vulnerable and dumb widows for as much money as possible. Only problem, Chung had rounded up a couple of widows who, though vulnerable, weren't dumb. Clarence swore he knew nothing about the demise of either Gladys or Leonard.

Chung was a different story. He pleaded ignorance of everything until someone arrived in the interrogation room and showed him a small pistol safely stowed in an evidence bag. The search warrant had turned up the pistol behind the grating of a heating vent in Chung's back room, and Thursday assured him that if the bullets in the gun matched the bullet taken from the chest of

Leonard and the fingerprints on the gun matched the fingerprints on Chung's fingers... story over. Chung caved like a Mississippi riverbank after a rainstorm. (I'd watched a movie on TCM about riverboats the week before.) Leonard had jumped the starting gate and tried to rob the widow Gladys in her apartment, and his abject failure had threatened to put an end to Chung's scheme to accumulate a long list of love-starved widows with money to dispense, so Leonard became a liability and instantly expendable. Leonard's attempted robbery had not turned out well for anyone involved.

Chung had come across the 1946 book about transcendentalism, his how-to manual as it were, which the police also found in the heating vent next to the gun, and he'd had his own kind of "insight." He appropriated the author's name, memorized a bunch of mumbo jumbo from the book, learned how to spell transcendentalism, and set out to get rich. It didn't turn out as he planned because my insight trumped his insight.

Feeling I'd had one of the better days of my private eye career, I put the *Boone's* back in the bottom drawer of my desk when Henny suggested dinner at the bar in Giandos. We were about to make our getaway as Henny stood in front of the mirror fussing with his fedora when someone knocked on our door.

"Awfully late for a client," he said.

"Go see. We're on a roll."

Henny threw me a thumbs-up, and a few seconds later, a one-armed man entered our office. I didn't realize right away he had only one arm, but when he sloughed off his heavy coat and handed it to Henny, I saw the right sleeve of his sports jacket tucked into the jacket's right pocket. He stood about my height, a couple inches short of six feet, had stringy, brown hair, and looked to be about fifty. I offered him our client chair, which I moved in front of Henny's desk. When we were situated, I asked the gentleman's name.

"Bob Elias."

"I'm Lloyd. He's Henny. What can we do for you?"

"It appears you were getting ready to leave. I apologize for arriving so late in the day, but I've been going back and forth over whether consulting you is the best thing to do."

"And you've decided it is?" I asked, offering a friendly smile.

"It is if I want to prevent a murder."

"A murder?" Henny snapped.

"Yes, a murder."

I asked, "Whose murder are you trying to prevent."

"My own."

Henny and I glanced at one another. "Perhaps you'd better explain," I suggested.

"You have time now? I don't want to throw a monkey wrench into your evening."

"Your problem sounds like there's an immediacy to it," Henny said. "I mean… your murder?"

Bob Elias gave a short chuckle. "No, they won't come after me tonight. I haven't officially announced yet."

"Go on," Henny urged. "Announced what?"

"My candidacy for city council. One of the Queens seats."

Elias sounded overly casual about an alarming situation, so I said, "I know people fight hard for political… shall we call it authority?"

"No, call it what it is. Power. Brute force."

"Okay, they fight hard for political power, but murder? Over a city council seat?"

"There's a back story. It'll take a while to tell."

"Have you had your dinner?" Henny asked.

Elias looked surprised. "No, no I haven't."

Henny looked my way. "Take him to Giandos?"

I thought it a rather extravagant way to treat a prospective client, but I was hungry and didn't want to put the man off and perhaps lose the business. On the other hand, since, according to him, it involved a possible murder, maybe there were others better able to handle such a situation. But we'd been on a good streak lately, so I agreed.

"Sure."

"Then you'll take me on as a client?"

Henny answered. "We'll need to hear your story first."

"I understand, but I must pay for my own dinner. I can't be accepting gifts from anybody. You know what the opposition and the newspapers can turn that into. You'll be on my security team, for the record."

"Okay with us," Henny said. "Let's go find a cab."

~ * ~

Henny and I sat Bob Elias between us at the bar. He commented on the spectacular view through the wall of windows, and after he ordered a Johnny Walker Black neat, I pretty much assumed the three of us would get along nicely, even though Henny and I stayed with wine. We told Roderigo to hold off on the menus for a while to give Elias time to unload his story on us.

"You're wondering about this, no doubt," he began, indicating his flaccid sleeve. "Iraq. Morgan Mitchell, you know the name?"

"Businessman, right? In the papers now and then? Isn't he talking about running for mayor?" I asked. "A Republican, isn't he?"

"Yep. He was my captain in Iraq."

Henny asked, "So you're running for city council to help him out?"

"No, anything but." Elias gave a sigh. "Is this... are we... like a lawyer-client relationship? Thoroughly confidential?"

"As far as we're concerned, it's confidential," Henny assured him.

I nodded my agreement but added a caution. "We do have access to an excellent reporter on the *Post*. In case there's anything that needs to be aired."

"No, no reporters yet," Elias insisted, wagging a cautionary finger, and we agreed. Susan would understand. "Morgan stole the freakin' army blind. I don't know how much he made on the black market, but he was the go-to guy where we were stationed. He spread things around among the unit, so nobody made a fuss, especially since everybody who was there hated being there, but..." He sipped some scotch. "...but I didn't go for it. There we were after 9/11 trying to right a wrong, achieve justice, settle a score, and all Morgan could think of was ripping off the army and making money."

"How did he... I mean, where could you spend money over there?" Henny asked.

"Not many places. I'm sure he sent it home."

"How in the world could he do that?" I asked. "Aren't there any guardrails for that kind of thing?"

"There are but money makes the guardrails pliable," Elias explained. "I don't know how much he siphoned off and sent through underground channels to...wherever. I said 'home,' but I don't know where the money ended up. The Caymans? Switzerland? Jersey City?"

"The things history doesn't tell you," Henny muttered. "I wonder if crap like that went on during World War II?"

"It goes on anywhere money is dumped in a big pile," Elias assured us. "And now he wants to run New York City. He ran a local school board in the Bronx when they had local schoolboards. I've done my research. Do you know how much double-billing, hell, even triple billing goes on when things are chopped into pieces as small as local school boards? Buy books someplace and send the bill to the city, the state, and the Feds. They pay and whoever is running the deal pockets two checks and pays for the books with the other. That is what Mitchell is a master at. How about we order some food, and then I'll tell you part two?"

After we ordered, Elias took up his story again. "I didn't go for this behavior in Iraq. It didn't remotely sit right with me. I wasn't around the Bronx when Mitchell cleaned up there, but I'm damn sure not going to let him have free run of the city treasury. I don't know why he doesn't move to Switzerland to be near his money and relax. He's gotta be at least sixty, sixty-five years old."

I thought of Susan. "You could go over your story with the reporter friend of ours. Blow the lid off."

"No, Mitchell'd quash the story somehow. Money can do wonders. I want to be the one... Look, my arm. I read Morgan, Captain Mitchell, the riot act in Iraq. I don't mean to sound all red-white-and-blue, but it really ticked me off. People were getting body parts blown off, and Morgan's only concern was when the next shipment of supplies was due in and how much could he skim off the top. Next thing I knew, I was leading squads cleaning out buildings, strongholds in the next town we were directed to. I threatened Mitchell... there really wasn't a lot I could threaten him with, but he was afraid I'd find my way to someone who would actually care about what he was doing. He had me lead a raid on a heavily fortified building and the next thing I knew, I was flat on my back in a hospital..." He gestured to his missing arm. "I want to be the one to take him down, and to do that I need to be inside of the tent with access to hard evidence. Your reporter friend may come in handy in time, but I want to have a council seat and make Morgan worry. Thing is, someone fired a shot at me two nights ago. It missed. I'm pretty sure it was meant to miss. The next day I got a call from Morgan saying he'd heard I planned to run for city council. I told him I was considering it. He said one word to me before he hung up. 'Don't.'"

A moment of silence ensued. Finally, Henny said, "We don't usually provide the kind of protection you're going to need."

"I'll have protection. I have campaign money. I can hire security. I'll list you as security. I want you to dig into Morgan Mitchell and either prove he's responsible for the threat to me or find out something maybe your reporter friend could use to blow him out of the water. I want it to be me blowing him out of the water, but any demolition would satisfy me in the end. So, what do you think?"

Two waiters arrived, hands full, balancing our dinners in front of them.

"Think it over while you eat," Elias advised.

I asked one of the waiters to move my dinner supplies next to Henny so he and I could talk, and after we had a short discussion between bites of chicken rollatini, we didn't see any reason not to get aboard the Bob Elias bandwagon.

When the waiter cleared our dishes, I returned to my spot next to Elias, who appeared in no hurry to leave. In fact, he ordered another scotch, this time Glenlivet, a single malt. I hesitate to call him a two-fisted drinker... sorry... but he certainly liked his scotch. While we were eating, he'd stepped away twice to talk on his cell. Now, he was going on about what his former captain would do to the finances of New York City if he ever got into power.

"He likely wants one more swing at the pinata before he disappears to enjoy his riches," Elias said, and I noted Henny's eyes go wide. I sat facing the end of the bar toward the rear wall and windows of the restaurant. Henny faced the entrance on the right and the spread of tables across the floor. For a moment I thought something bad had happened, but Henny's eyes softened, and I made a good guess at what had caught his attention. I looked over my shoulder and a lovely young woman had stepped into sight. She'd obviously checked her coat in the lobby and stood smiling our way. She wore a tight, solid blue dress, which stopped short at midthigh. Her shoulders and arms were exposed, and her light brown hair hung loosely to her shoulders. I looked back at Henny as the young woman came toward us. She stretched out her arms and wrapped them around Bob Elias. I could see the instant change in Henny's attitude when she said, "Hi, Daddy." Henny knocked his chair askew when he stood up to welcome her.

"Here," he offered. "Sit next to your... father. I'll move over one."

I could sense Henny crossing his fingers, hoping that her "Daddy" actually meant daddy and wasn't a creepy term of affection for her lover.

"Gentlemen," Elias said, getting to his feet without the clumsy drama of Henny's move, "let me introduce you to my daughter, Darla. Darla, this is Henny, and this is Lloyd."

Henny held the bar chair for Darla as we managed to get back in order.

"Would you like something?" Henny asked. He turned and beckoned Roderigo.

"Oh, maybe a chardonnay," she said, beaming a grateful smile Henny's way.

"You didn't have to come out here," Elias said.

"I like to come and get you and take you home," she said softly. "You know I like to do that."

"She takes good care of me," Elias said. "Too good care of me."

"I like to see him at home, safe and sound at the end of the day," she explained, making a clear effort to keep the conversation light. "How many is that?" Darla asked, indicating her father's scotch.

"Only two. Corroborate that for me, fellows?"

We corroborated and Darla seemed satisfied.

"These men are private detectives, sweetie. They're going to help me get a city council seat. Be right back. I need to go recycle the scotch."

When Elias disappeared into the lobby, Darla said, "He's insistent on running for the city council. He's told you all of that, it seems?"

"Yes," Henny replied. "He also seems to have it in for the former captain he served under in Iraq."

"He did serve in Iraq, didn't he?" I added, beginning to have some doubts about this entire situation.

"Oh, yes. It changed him. Physically, as you can see and... otherwise. Of course, I didn't know him before Iraq. My mother left long ago. She's out in Oregon. But I don't like to leave him on his own too much. Sometimes he gets... ideas."

I didn't know how to phrase it, but I tried. "He's not... uh, you know... mentally damaged...?"

"No, no. Not really." She looked down for a moment. "Iraq was difficult for him, I know. But he's able to live his life. He does quite well. He lives on his own, no problem. He gets a healthy disability payment. He works two days a week answering the phone in a real-estate office. No, he's okay."

I spoke quickly, hoping Elias wouldn't reappear and end my chance to question his daughter. "He came to us this afternoon and told us he believes this captain..." I looked at Henny. "...Morgan Mitchell?"

"That's the name," Henny confirmed.

"This Morgan Mitchell is a bad man. Had it in for him in Iraq and is a thief ready to wreak havoc on New York City finances if he gets to be mayor."

"He doesn't tell me much about Iraq, but he does often tell me this Mr. Mitchell is a bad man, but he's a Republican in New York City. What chance do you think he's got to be elected mayor?"

I thought for a moment. "Probably not much."

"Exactly. Dad talks to me about politics a lot. I'm not all that interested, but I listen. Iraq, though, had to have been an absolute nightmare for him..." Darla's voice caught but, thankfully, Elias turned the corner from the lobby. He stopped to speak with Roderigo for a moment, and Darla used the opportunity to scribble something—her phone number it turned out—on a bar napkin with a pen she pulled from her purse, and she passed the napkin to Henny. "Please, talk to me."

Elias rejoined us and after a few minutes Darla suggested that she and her father head for home.

"Gentlemen," Elias said. "Consider yourself on the payroll. We'll talk tomorrow. I have your card."

Darla eyed Henny and made the same request with her eyes. Henny gave a sly nod. We watched father and daughter head into the lobby, then returned to what was left of our wine.

"One more?" Henny asked.

"This is getting complicated," I said. "Sure." Roderigo refilled our glasses. "I didn't get a chance to ask her about the bullet fired at her father. Did it happen? Is Elias making this stuff up?"

"I'll call her tomorrow and ask."

"She's pretty, isn't she?"

"Seems like a nice person, too. Don't worry. I'll call her."

I wasn't worried. I knew he would.

Twenty-six

I woke up in a bad mood the next morning. Bob Elias, when he walked into the office and during our time in Giandos before his daughter showed up, seemed like a real catch for Henny and me. A war hero with a moral nature a mile wide. Then his daughter arrived. His keeper. In the bright light of the new dawn, Elias seemed to have no more chance of being elected to New York's city council than Henny did of tossing his fedora onto a prong of our coat stand and making it stick. He'd pay us out of campaign funds? He'd save the city treasury from being ransacked by big, bad Morgan Mitchell, who'd stolen the Department of Defense blind during the Iraq war? It seemed dubious at best.

Still lying in bed, I texted Henny to ask Darla about her father's finances. And was he really a candidate for high office? And were we actually hired for anything at all? Henny, responding to his over-generous heart, might want to help the Elias family, but I didn't see any benefit to wasting our time feeding Bob Elias's fantasies and delusions. Especially for no money.

Henny texted back he'd ask Darla what the real situation was. I got out of bed and put myself together. An hour later I was behind my office desk reading about Nero Wolfe when Henny arrived.

"So, what's up?" I asked as I slid Nero Wolfe into my desk drawer. "Did you make the call?"

"I did." Henny had reached his desk chair, taken off his dark fedora, and sailed it toward the coat rack. Then he went, picked the hat up from the floor, and hung it next to his coat.

"And?"

"Let me get some coffee first. Want a donut?"

He dropped a white paper bag on my desk, and I fished out a glazed donut.

Finally, Henny reported. "She claims her father is usually quite normal, a regular guy. He watches Mets and Giants games. Follows the Knicks. But he's got a glaring obsession about this Morgan Mitchell."

"Then he really did go to war and this Mitchell was his captain?"

"Darla says yes. And the missing arm. Arms don't simply fall off, you know."

"Right, the arm. That couldn't've been easy. I'd be nuts too... Never mind. What else did she say?"

"Her father attends meetings of the Queens Reform Democratic Club. Card-carrying member, as the phrase goes. So, he is somewhat involved in politics."

"Is he running for city council?"

"Uh, not unless the club puts him up for consideration to the movers and shakers."

"Darla said?"

"She did."

"Not much chance of that, I imagine."

Henny shrugged. "Lost an arm in war. Claims to be very anti-corruption. The Dems could do worse."

"More to the point. Does he have a campaign war chest from which he can pay our fee?"

"He does not."

"Darla said?"

"Darla said."

"I figured as much."

"But Darla wants to hire us."

I frowned. I knew Henny's soft-heartedness would get us entwined in this fantasy cluster love-in somehow. "To do what?"

"She's worried he'll run his mouth too much in public. Morgan Mitchell is a real person, a *serious* person. And he *does* have a campaign war chest... *filled* with money."

"And he definitely served in Iraq with Elias?"

"Darla assured me they served together, and he was a captain. And Elias does have a years-long thing about the man. She's afraid her father will go too far."

"Does she think he's in danger. Does she know about the bullet he says came his way?"

"I asked. She does know about it, but she doesn't believe it. She thinks her father made up the story to convince her of the seriousness of the situation and the need for him to run for office to set things right."

"Jeez, Elias is a few votes short of a majority." I tapped my temple.

"Darla doesn't have a lot of money..." Here it comes, I thought. "...but she can give us a thousand bucks a month to keep an eye on her father until his club chooses to pass along someone else's name to the party for consideration as a candidate. By the way, she tells me no one his Democratic club has ever recommended has made it onto the actual ballot."

"And how long will this assignment last? We need to earn a living, you know." I admire Henny's good heartedness. I really do.

But I also admire having enough money to eat, drink, and pay the rent. I knew where Henny's intentions were heading. "So, are you seeing her soon?"

Henny took a long time sipping his coffee. "It'll last maybe a month or so. There are details we need to... to flesh out."

"Flesh out? Freudian slip?"

"No, no. She's nice. She deserves our help, don't you think?"

Henny'd had such poor luck with women, I didn't have the heart to fuss over the matter. I'm good hearted, too, so I agreed. "Sure. Where are you taking her?"

"Who said I'm taking her anywhere?"

"I'm a detective, remember?"

"Right. I forgot. We've having dinner tomorrow night."

"So, what do we do until then? We're on her payroll, right? Do we follow her father around?"

"I've given that some thought, and no, she didn't ask us to follow her father around."

"Go on."

"I think you should suggest to Susan that she interview Morgan Mitchell. A simple interview shouldn't generate any suspicion toward Elias. Why would it? Mitchell's running for office. He wants publicity. Maybe she can work something about Mitchell's time in Iraq into their conversation. It's possible Elias knows what he's talking about, and Susan will uncover a giant story of fraud."

"Do you want to ask Susan or shall I?"

"You."

I laughed. "Okay. I'll let you know what she says."

~ * ~

I thought back and wondered why I'd laughed when I told Henny I'd ask Susan about interviewing Morgan Mitchell. She would surely ask me why I was suggesting the interview, and Henny and I had taken a vow of silence to Bob Elias not to repeat what he'd told us to a reporter, in other words, to Susan. 'Quandary,' I believe, is the word I'm looking for. I mentioned it to Henny later in the day, and he assured me I'd figure it out. Yeah, thanks.

The next word I looked for was 'equivocate.' It turned out to be a good word, a necessary word, so I equivocated.

"How did you come up with that suggestion?" Susan asked me as we lay in our own beds that night, chatting over our cells.

"We got a new client today who's thinking of running for city council, and we got talking politics. The *Post* likes Republicans. Morgan Mitchell's a Republican running for mayor. Seemed a natural for you. Even if you can't use the story now, it'll come in handy closer to the primary. I'll come with you to the interview. Schedule it in the late afternoon if you can. We can lay off afterward, have dinner, make an evening out of it."

"So, we'll have a romantic interview with a man who can't possibly be elected our next mayor? Sounds wonderful."

"Never say never. Pataki won; Rockefeller was a Republican; Guiliani, whatever he was."

Susan laughed and said, "Why not? What's your new client's name?"

"Bob Elias."

"Never heard of him. Why'd he hire you?"

"For security. Probably just to travel around with him."

"Doesn't sound very specific. And security means you'll probably have to carry a gun."

Henny and I had only once been involved in something that forced us to go armed, and Henny had actually fired a bullet, albeit into a loaded trash bag.

"Yeah, I guess it does."

"I don't know if I like that."

"Hey, Henny and I are hard-nosed detectives. Besides, Elias is only a minor player. Not even double A league. He'll likely drop out before things even get going. And I get the unhappy impression he doesn't have much money. When he stops paying us, he'll be on his own."

Susan gave a modestly acquiescent grunt, then agreed to set up the interview. Three cheers for equivocation.

~ * ~

Henny and I closed the office at three-thirty on Tuesday. He went home for a nap and after his nap to get himself ready for dinner with Darla Elias. I met Susan downstairs on Centre Street for an Uber ride to Queens.

Morgan Mitchell's campaign headquarters was on the ground floor of a small building located between a restaurant calling itself the Crab House and a large, decrepit factory building which offered two tennis courts for the athletically minded. We entered and identified ourselves to a young man who sat at a long table stuffing campaign literature into envelopes.

"You're doing it the old-fashioned way, I see," Susan said, beaming a smile his way.

The man frowned. "I don't know why. We can reach a lot more people for a lot less money over social media."

Susan offered a rationale. "Maybe these envelopes go to people who can actually vote. Unlike social media."

The young man shrugged. Adding a scowl, he added, "Maybe. Mr. Mitchell is not of the internet generation. He's expecting you." He pointed to a door in the corner of the room. "Let me text him you're here. He knows how to do that much, at least." A moment passed. "You can go in."

"If Mitchell has seven aides, we can name this one Grumpy," I said as we walked to the office door.

"Must be a *paid* campaign worker," Susan said with a laugh. "Otherwise, he'd be off somewhere else."

Morgan Mitchell sat behind a desk and rose when we entered. Susan introduced us—me as her research assistant. Mitchell was somewhat bowling ball shaped. He had very little neck, and if he were dressed in a white suit, I'd be forced to attach 'snowman-like' to a description of him. He retained a healthy mop of gray hair.

Susan did all the talking from our side of the desk and jotted down things on a notepad as necessary. After half an hour she and Mitchell had run out of steam. On the way to Mitchell's headquarters in Susan's Uber, I'd made a point of letting her know I wanted to ask him some questions, mostly about Iraq. From the look she gave me, I realized my skills at equivocation were running thin.

"Is there something you're not telling me?" she asked.

"Well... reporters have their code of ethics and detectives do, too. Don't worry. You'll be the first to know."

She knew she would be, so the moment passed.

"Lloyd," Susan said. "You have some questions, I believe?"

"I do." I heard the click of Susan's pen as she got ready to write. My stomach did a nervous little dance, and I cleared my throat. "Yes, thanks. Mr. Mitchell, you mentioned that you served in Iraq."

"I did."

"Can you tell me more about what your experience was like?"

"Sure. Have you got a couple of hours?"

I gave an understanding chuckle, and my stomach hurt a little more. "I guess the question was overly broad. More about your responsibilities there?"

"Aside from killing bad guys?"

"If you had other responsibilities, sure. I'm certain the newspaper's readers—the voters— would be interested in hearing about them." I felt like I was offering him a helping of weak pablum spiced with gobbledygook.

"Supply security was where they put me. I suggest you read over my campaign bio. I received a medal for what I did. Protecting our supplies was as much a part of the war as anything else. And it was a place where security started out almost non-existent. No sooner did we get a shipment of supplies than stuff would start marching out the door like it was late for a meeting. I put a quick stop to crap like that. Iraqis, some of our own soldiers, didn't matter who. I could understand people needing survival money and having to deal with the black market. In the beginning, our arms, our food, everything they sent us, some of it always ended up for sale somewhere else, if you knew where to look. I cracked down hard." Mitchell ran his tongue across his lips. I glanced at Susan. I could see in her eyes what I felt, too. Mitchell's emotions had been engaged. "Real hard to enforce, but I enforced it. If I caught one of our own fooling around, I shipped him to another outfit or kept him so busy going out on patrol, he got the message. Made a boatload of enemies, and I had to keep eyes front and back wherever I went, but it got the job done." The moment broke and Mitchell readjusted his posture. "That's all you need to know about that. Read the bio. Anything else?"

I shot another arrow into the air. "Were there any major blowups over the supplies going to the black market?"

"Weren't you listening to me? What are you after? This is ancient history. I'll tell you again. I was given a medal for my work keeping a watch over the supplies. It's time, way past time, for someone to do the same for New York City's supply chain." He got to his feet. "I hope I've given you enough material. Now, I've got work to do and an election to win."

"One more question," I said. "Was your election to the local school board your first venture into elective politics?"

"School board? I was never on any school board. Where'd you hear that?" Mitchell looked at Susan. "I hope you're the one writing this story."

Susan assured him she would be the author of the article. We both thanked him and wished him well. We left his office and said goodbye to the young man still stuffing envelopes. I asked him for a campaign biography, and he pushed one of the papers he'd been stuffing my way. I thanked him. He grunted a grim farewell, and five minutes later, Susan's Uber pulled up, and we headed back to Manhattan and Bocca di Bacco for an early dinner.

Twenty-seven

I caved early, in fact midway through the first glass of wine. Susan knew I was holding something back from her. I knew she knew I was holding out, and I simply caved. I started with Bob Elias walking into the office and went through everything from then till now. I could feel the elastic band of amity between Susan and me, which had stretched to a point of noticeable tension, relax and return to its default pliancy. I explained about Henny being the only one I could talk to about the case, but how she often helped in ways Henny couldn't. Plus, I admitted feeling unduly and unnecessarily pressured to keep my pledge to Elias not to take the case to a reporter. Susan, in her glorious, wonderful way, put me at my ease.

"Lloyd, darling, then let's say you're talking to me as, we'll call it a friend, and not as a reporter. Naturally, I will keep your confidence."

I lifted my half-filled wineglass to her, and we clicked. I liked this woman.

"So," she continued, "Elias claims Mitchell was a thief and wanted to kill him to prevent him from being a whistleblower. Mitchell claims he was the savior, not the abuser, of the supplies that came into... into camp, and he protected the supplies from people like Elias, although not Elias specifically. Sound right?"

"You've nailed it. Henny's out with Darla tonight. I'll be interested in their topics of conversation."

"How did Elias strike you when you spoke with him?"

"Like I said, he seemed reasonable until Darla showed up and gave us a quick lesson in her father's disabilities. I don't know what to make of things. Elias is delusional. There's no city council seat in his future. I think we can agree on that." I waited for a reaction, and Susan bobbed her head twice. "So... there we are. Darla's willing to humor her father..."

"To the tune of a thousand dollars a month."

"Yep." I shrugged. "But likely only for one month. Let's eat. I'll fill you in on Henny's night as soon as he fills me in. I'm glad I talked to you about this."

Susan arched an eyebrow and said, "So am I."

That elastic band of amity had given a quiver but remained soft and yielding.

~ * ~

I knew better than to phone Henny when I got home and disturb anything he might be involved in, and he didn't call me. He did precede me into the office next morning, a rare occurrence.

"How'd it go?" I asked. I noticed Henny's fedora on the floor next to the coat stand. I picked it up and hung it on a prong. Then I proceeded to the coffee machine.

"It was good," Henny said.

He already had a spread of toothpicks in front of him as well as one jutting from between his lips.

"So, the two of you got along okay?"

"We did."

"Did her father come up in conversation?"

Henny made a puffing sound. "Did he come up? Nothing *but* him came up."

I sat and spun my chair to face Henny. "How so?"

"Well, with her constant talking about him, she didn't come right out and say it, but she's obviously worried about him. He's lucid and intelligent most of the time, but when he gets on politics and his fairy tale city council ambitions, he... and I quote her... 'he goes off the deep end.'"

"Meaning?"

"Meaning she gets hazy when she goes there. She wasn't at all hazy when she told me how much time he spent with her when she was little. Playing with her, taking her places. She said when she was three or four, she thought men with two arms were unusual. Something was wrong with *them*, not her dad."

"She mention her mother leaving for Oregon?"

"Yeah, yeah. Her father started getting overwrought about politics and especially about this Morgan Mitchell, and finally, her mother couldn't take it any longer."

"How'd Elias end up with Darla? Why didn't she go to Oregon with Mom?"

"Darla was a senior in high school and didn't want to relocate for her graduation. She ended up staying in New York for college because she'd always lived here and because of her father. She realized how much he needed her. She feels better having him under her eye."

"Quite the devoted daughter."

"She is."

"And?"

"And what?"

"Are you going to see her again? I mean socially."

"Sure. Be nice if she expanded her conversational topics, though. We'll see. I like her."

"Did you two discuss anything about our assignment?"

"She said she'll call us when she wants us to do something regarding her father."

"And we still get paid if she doesn't call us?"

"I suppose."

Henny's cell chimed and he answered. He looked my way, eyebrows raised, and said, "I had a nice night too. Thanks."

Darla. I listened to Henny set up a tentative appointment. When he ended the call he said, "Darla wants to bring Dad in this afternoon or tomorrow morning. He got an invitation to some kind of political thing. She wasn't too clear. She said she hasn't had a chance to discuss it with her father yet. She gets nervous when he gets amped up about politics. She'll call me."

Darla called Henny back around three and said she and her father would show up on Centre Street tomorrow morning, but she'd call ahead. It reminded me to tell Henny I'd cracked and brought Susan fully into the case.

"I figured it was only a matter of time," Henny said. "I'm glad you did. Usually, she's smarter than the two of us put together."

That sentiment irked me, not because Henny said it but because it was probably true. At any rate, we now had three crack minds working on the Bob Elias case. What could go wrong?

~ * ~

Darla phoned the next morning around ten and showed up with her father a few minutes past one. I moved my desk chair to the other side of my desk and used a metal folding chair for myself. I offered bottles of water around but got no takers. Henny, naturally, took the lead.

"So, what's up? How can we help you?"

Both father and daughter commenced speaking at the same time. They turned and stared at one another. Darla tipped her head toward her father.

"Thank you," he said, then addressed Henny and me. "I've been invited to a meeting where Morgan Mitchell is scheduled to speak, and I want to hear what the rat has to say. If he portrays himself as a righteous, honest, guardian of the people, I'll get up and denounce him. I'll tell the truth about him. I'll settle him for all time."

"Dad, please," Darla petitioned. "How Dad got this invitation, I can't explain. Even though it says all are welcome, it seems to be a strictly Republican-oriented meeting." She turned to her father. "What mailing list were you on...?"

"I'm on a lot of mailing lists," Elias interrupted. "And good thing I am if I can put a stop to Mitchell's bull..."

"Dad! Stop. He'll be there preaching to the converted. It's not the appropriate forum for what you're talking about."

"Hold on, hold on," I put in. "Listen..." I waited for the Elias family to sit back and take a breath. "I have met Mitchell."

"What!" Elias burst out. "How, why, where?"

He couldn't get his interrogatives out fast enough. I held up my hand and began a careful explanation. "I accompanied a reporter who was doing a story on him. As a man running for mayor, he's a story. You'll agree with me there, I know." I kept talking, hoping no one would mention my pledge of silence. "She went to interview him, and I tagged along."

"What's your point?" Darla asked.

"My point is this. I probably shouldn't have... not my place... but I threw in a couple questions of my own, with the reporter's permission, of course. I asked him about his Iraq experience. He tells it another way, Mr. Elias. He paints himself as the protector of the supplies, rather than the bandit you claim."

"Of course he does," Elias cried. "Would he be stupid enough to do otherwise?" Elias waved his one arm for emphasis. "I'm going to go to the meeting and listen to him. When he sees me, he'll likely be too embarrassed to bring up the topic of his past or lie about it. If he does tell lies, and I get a chance, I'll shut him down quick. I hope they allow public comment."

"Dad, this isn't good for you. It upsets you. I don't like to see you this way."

"I'm going." He dramatically buttoned his lip.

"Then I'm going with you, and I want these two gentlemen to come along, too."

"I don't care what you folks do. I'm going."

Henny spoke up. "When and where is this meeting?"

"This Saturday night in a private room in the Crab House restaurant next to Mitchell's election headquarters in Queens."

"I know where it is," I said. "The interview I went to took place in his headquarters."

"Darla," Henny said, rising, "we'll be there. What time does it happen?"

"Seven o'clock."

"It's in a private room, you say? Lloyd and I will meet you inside the restaurant at six-thirty. We'll go into the meeting together. You said everyone's welcome, right? We won't need an invitation?"

"No. We don't need a specific invitation."

"Okay, then. No problem."

I got to my feet, too, to help Henny along in clearing the room. Our guests took the hint and stood. Elias had nothing more to say, but Darla thanked us and gave Henny a meaningful look. She was depending on him... on us... to keep her father within bounds. At least that's how I read it. Henny walked them to the door and said, "Don't worry, Darla. Lloyd and I will be there." She smiled and they left.

~ * ~

Naturally, I let Susan know the latest, and naturally, she insisted on coming along to the meeting, so on Saturday, Susan picked up Henny and me, and we Ubered to Queens and the Crab House. We settled in at the end of the bar nearest the entrance and ordered beers. It was the kind of bar where ordering beer came with the territory. I felt we'd have gotten looks if we ordered wine. A belt-high wooden wall separated the bar from the restaurant tables, which were maybe half occupied. The noise level was low. A few people disappeared through a rear doorway into a room where I presumed the meeting would take place.

"Quarter of," Henny said. "Where are they?"

On cue, Darla and Bob Elias stepped into the restaurant. Darla helped her father off with his overcoat and hung it and her own coat on one of the half dozen stands lined up against one wall. Darla wore a green pantsuit and her father had on his usual sports jacket, the right sleeve tucked neatly into the pocket. They'd spotted us as soon as they entered, and after dealing with their coats, they joined us.

Henny gave Darla a smile. "I was getting worried."

Darla frowned and offered no reason for being fifteen minutes behind.

"Let's go in," Elias said. "I want a seat where I can hear everything."

Henny tossed money on the bar, and we made our way to the meeting room. It had nearly filled up. I counted ten rows of chairs with twelve chairs in a row. Elias led us up the left side to the second row. He and Darla took the first two seats, Elias on the outside. Henny and I sat behind them while Susan wandered off. Not everyone was seated and through the mingling mob, I spotted Morgan Mitchell, a politician's smile on his face, shaking hands with whomever cared to do so. Little by little, people found their seats, and the room looked to be two-thirds full. A lectern faced the rows of chairs, elevated maybe six inches from the floor atop a broad box with two folding chairs, one on each side of the lectern, where Mitchel finally sat along with a gentleman who would no doubt run the meeting. At seven-ten, things had gotten into enough order that the man sitting next to Mitchell rose.

"Okay, folks, still chairs in back. We'll get started in a minute or two." He stepped away and bent to speak with Mitchell.

I sat on the aisle in back of Elias while Henny took the chair behind Darla. Susan wandered about in the rear of the room, interviewing whoever would talk to her. The host moved behind the lectern.

"I'm George Handelman, campaign manager. Nice to see so many of you here for this important meeting." Handelman gestured toward his seated guest. "We have... we have..." He held up his hands and the room finally quieted. I spotted Susan standing against the far side wall. "We have with us tonight, Morgan Mitchell." A round of polite applause circled the room. Elias's head went left and right slowly. "As you know, Morgan has been a force in this city for years and is going to be the next mayor of New York City." Another round of applause, this one stronger than the first, traveled the room. "That's right. And he needs our help. Politics is about bettering the lives of the people you represent..." The host smiled. "...but it's also about money." A twittering laugh filled a few seconds. "Morgan is going to speak to you, but I'll take a moment to point out the small table in the corner..." The host stretched out his arm. "The campaign accepts checks, cash, whatever you can spare. But you're here to listen to Morgan, not to me, so without further ado, ladies and gentlemen, the next mayor of our great city, Morgan Mitchell."

Mitchell rose, bearing his campaign smile, as more applause greeted him. He waved to a few people and nodded to certain others. Handelman took a seat and crossed his legs.

"Thank you, thank you." The crowd quieted for Mitchell. "Some of you know me, and I'm sure I'm new to others of you. You can pick up my campaign biography and a short essay on what I stand for at the table George pointed out, as well as from Larry as you go out the door."

Larry looked to be the young fellow I'd seen stuffing envelopes. He looked no happier tonight than he had then. "Let me begin by telling you I've proudly served our country," Mitchell went on.

Elias stiffened, his head upright and still.

"I am not bragging when I say I received commendations for the time I served in Iraq. They're listed in my bio..."

Then all hell broke loose.

Elias was on his feet and took a step to his left into the aisle. He shouted, "You ruined everything," then withdrew a small pistol from his left pocket, pointed it toward the dais and fired twice. I felt a sharp pain in my foot as Henny trod on it as he flew by me and took Elias to the floor. Henny's whizzing past me combined with the bolt of pain woke me up, and I saw him on Elias's back, holding him by the shoulders. They rolled over and I saw the gun still in Elias's hand, Henny trying to latch onto Elias's wrist or arm. I leaped into the aisle and fell in a crush onto my knees on top of Elias's wrist. He screamed and so did Henny. People in the audience were shouting. A few men held Elias down. Two people sat on his legs and others fought for the chance to grab him anywhere else. When I landed on the gun-toting wrist, the gun dropped free. I grabbed for it and knew enough to get the safety latched. Then I got to my feet, put the gun into my pants pocket—it was that small—and pulled Henny away from the shooter—there were plenty of others to hold onto him.

"You freakin' broke my arm," Henny barked at me, pain etched across his face. "What did you do?"

"I jumped on his arm."

"My arm was under his arm. Oh, sweet Jesus, it hurts. Did he get Mitchell?"

In the hubbub, I'd forgotten the purpose of Elias's attack. I looked at the dais and saw Mitchell in one chair and Handelman in the other, both pressing towels to themselves, Handelman to the right side of his head and Mitchell to his left shoulder. The crazy thought went through me that it was a good thing Elias was right-handed and had to shoot with his off hand. I don't know why I thought that since I had no idea whether Elias was right- or left-handed.

Through the babble in the room, I picked up sirens growing louder. I looked where I'd last seen Susan but found she'd made her way nearer the dais. Our eyes met and I flashed a thumbs-up. She nodded and went back to work.

To Henny, I said, "Mitchell and the other guy are wounded but both are sitting in chairs. It doesn't look too bad."

"I see them. God, I gotta get my wrist taken care of. Two gunshot wounds and a smashed wrist. Guess who's going to be number three on the triage list?"

The sirens stopped and a moment later three policemen burst into the room and began ushering the attendees out. Right behind the police were white-suited medical people who went straight to the dais. I got the final medico's attention.

"We have a broken wrist over here," I said, not knowing whether Henny's wrist was broken or not, but I could not take the look of pain on my partner's face.

"Be right with you, pal."

I stayed close to the EMT, and when he saw there were enough of his colleagues to handle the two wounded men, I led him to Henny. He looked Henny over.

"Looks broken. Come with me."

"Want me with you?" I asked Henny.

"No, no. Take care of Susan and Darla. Find out what the hell went on here. And give the cop the gun. Don't go taking it home with you."

I turned over Elias's gun to one of the officers as the EMT took Henny out of the room.

Then I watched two police officers escort Bob Elias and Darla in the same direction.

The room now nearly empty, Susan flashed her *New York Post* reporter's ID to the remaining officer and took me under her wing. Handelman was already on his feet, bathing the side of his head above his right ear with a wet towel. Mitchell, the EMTs put on a stretcher, much contrary to his wishes, and both men trailed behind the others toward, I presumed, the ambulance whose siren I'd heard.

Susan said, "I'm going with the police officer." She pointed to a husky young fellow who barked orders to the remaining people to leave the room. "I'll get in touch with you as soon as I can. Let me call you an Uber. Go outside and look like you're waiting for an Uber." Susan went to stand next to the barking officer, and I, not knowing what else to do, left the meeting room. The restaurant proper had been cleared, and I followed Susan's directions. When she finally left the restaurant, escorted by the officer, she called to me, "It's a blue Rav 4. Keep an eye out for it."

Five minutes later, a blue Rav 4 pulled up near the restaurant and I identified myself. I couldn't think of anywhere to go except home. If I'd known where they'd taken Henny, I'd have gone there, but I didn't, and thirty minutes later, I was on my sofa, a healthy glass of *Boone's That's All* in my hand.

Twenty-eight

At two-thirty a.m. the notifications alert on my phone, which I'd purposely left on, beeped. I surfaced through my *Boone's* fog and saw a text from Henny telling me he was home and had a cast on his left wrist and would have for maybe four weeks. He felt fine but I shouldn't expect to see him in the office till the next afternoon when we would catch up. I went back to sleep and next morning I was at my desk by ten o'clock and got a lot of reading done.

A few minutes before three, Henny showed up, a shining, short, white cast on his left wrist. He held it up.

"Thanks," he said.

"You know you stepped on my foot when you went flying into the aisle."

"Oh, I did. Let me offer you my thoughts and prayers."

We both laughed. Henny's injury did not prevent him from dressing in his usual pinstriped, double-breasted suit and fedora, this time each a shade of gray. He tossed his hat toward the coat rack.

"You'd think the universe would compensate me some," he muttered as he bent to retrieve his hat. "So, what happened after I left?" He took his seat and spun his desk chair my way.

"You didn't miss anything," I reported. "Handelman has a scrape on his head." I touched above my right ear. "And Mitchell looked like he stepped out of an old cowboy movie. You know, wounded in the shoulder. They made him go out on a stretcher. Susan went along. I haven't heard from her yet." On cue, my cell made its noise. "Speak of the... woman."

I listened and got my orders.

"She wants to meet us in the San Remo." The San Remo was a semi-upscale pizza joint a block away. "She says she's hungry."

"Okay with me," Henny said. "I only nibbled for breakfast."

And off we went to the San Remo.

~ * ~

Both Henny and Susan ordered spaghetti and meatballs, something that would certainly stick to their ribs. I merely ordered two slices, plain.

Henny assured Susan he was feeling better. "The doctor said about four weeks before it comes off," he said, in response to a question from her.

"I had no choice," she said smiling, "but to write you up big in the story, both of you."

"I hope you didn't tell the world my partner broke my wrist by jumping on it," Henny said. "He tell you I stepped on his foot on my way to collar the shooter?"

I frowned. Susan laughed. "No, he didn't. Both of you subdued the gunman, and you, Henny, were hurt in the scuffle. That was my phrasing."

"How are the two victims?" I asked, hoping to change the subject.

"They had to take the bullet out of Mitchell's shoulder, so he went to sleep for a while, but he's patched up and after a few days off, he'll be back on the campaign trail. The publicity may do him good. You never know. The doctor told me if the bullet had been bigger, it would have gone right through the flesh, and he would only have needed to be patched up."

"There's your good news, bad news scenario in spades," Henny said.

"Anyway," Susan went on, "Mitchell really is the decorated GI he claims to be. He said Elias was one of those he kept assigning elsewhere to keep him away from the supplies. On one of his assignments, there was an accident—his arm."

"His arm and a good bit of his mind," Henny added.

"Well, he got disability, came home and married, had Darla, but with the passage of time, his state of mind deteriorated. You saw the result. Have you heard from Darla?"

Henny shook his head. "No, she left with her father, and I don't want to butt in for a while. I don't know what her opinion will be of the fellow who brought her father down." Our food came and we settled into idle chitchat.

Henny had just wiped the last vestiges of tomato sauce from his chin when his cell chimed. He checked, then looked up, wide-eyed. "Darla. I gotta take this." He got up and walked to a quiet corner.

"You're awfully quiet today," Susan said to me.

"I don't want any more nights like last night. Was Elias right- or left-handed?"

Susan shrugged. "I don't know. Why...? Oh, I see. Was he shooting with his good hand?"

"I wondered whether, you know, a little thing like that saved the lives of two men."

"Good point. I'll find out and put it in a follow up story if it's useful."

I glanced Henny's way. "He's smiling."

Susan turned to look. "Good sign. Oh, here he comes."

Henny reclaimed his chair.

"You look chipper, I said."

"Darla thanked me. She *thanked* me! She said I probably saved her father's life. She's already spoken with a lawyer who thinks the DA will likely suggest her father go to an institution..." He tapped his temple with a finger. "...rather than the lockup. She said he's been under psychological treatment a few times in the past."

"Better than going to prison, I suppose," I said.

"Much better," Susan agreed. "I'll keep track of that part of the story, too."

Henny rose. "Don't make me wait to read it in the newspaper. Call when you hear something definitive."

"Yes, sir. But do keep your eye on the *Post*. This is a big story. And it's *my* big story."

Susan ran her palm lovingly along my cheek. "Thanks to you two fellows. Gotta get back to it. Dinner and a sleepover sometime soon, love?"

"You bet," I agreed. We waited with Susan until her Uber arrived, then we walked back to the office. Going up the stairs to our floor—the elevator had momentarily broken down—I congratulated Henny.

"You seem to have made a big impression on Darla... you're a hero to her."

"I was thinking the same thing. On the phone, she said she'd take me to dinner when she felt she could leave her father on his own. Only a day or two, she promised."

We reached our office, and I unlocked the door. I entered first and before I reached my desk, Henny let out a whoop. I turned and followed his gaze. His fedora hung, still swaying, on one of the coat rack prongs.

"Did you do that?" I asked.

"I did! All the way from here!"

"My friend, between Darla and your fedora, I'd say your luck is changing for the better."

"It's about time."

"A quick *Boone's* to celebrate?"

"Absolutely."

"And to make up for breaking your wrist, and to keep your good luck flowing, the next two office bottles of *Boone's* are on me." I got out our current bottle and grabbed paper cups off the coffee maker tray.

I poured.

Henny toasted. "To the future."

We drank.

Meet John Paulits

John Paulits lives in New York City and spent many years there teaching. He has written fiction for over forty years, novels for children as well as adults. *Henny and Lloyd Fight Crime* is his twenty-second book for Wings ePress. To learn more about John's books, visit his author page at the Wings' website: www.wingsepress.com.

Other Works From The Pen Of John Paulits

For ages 8-12

Philip Gets Even—By accident at an art show in which they are entered, Philip Felton and Emery Wyatt offend Johnny Visco, the toughest boy in sixth grade, and he promises to get even. When Johnny Visco's attacks show no sign of stopping, Philip, Emery, and Mr. Conway concoct a plan that finally puts Johnny Visco in his place and prevents him from tormenting the boys any longer.

Philip and the Case of Mistaken Identity—
Philip and his best friend Emery, detectives on the trail, try to cope with a mystifying little girl who runs them a merry chase.

The Director— The Director invites nine-year-old Tommy Whitaker to be a character in a book set in 1957. The trouble begins in the Regal movie theatre, where after the Saturday matinee. Elwood Wambo, the strange caretaker of the movie theatre, hires Tommy and his 1957 best friend, Mouse, to stay behind on future Saturdays to clean the theatre when the movie is over. The boys later learn that Wambo and his partner Jeremy are part of a gang of thieves. When their friend Smitty's bike is stolen and when Smitty himself mysteriously disappears, Tommy and his two friends, Mouse and Royal, vow to solve the mysteries of their missing friend, his missing bike...and a murder.

A Cat Tale— Hayden and his fellow cats find their way to paradise: TALULA TUPPERMAN'S HOME FOR DISTRESSED FELINES. But Rodney and Stanley, cat kidnappers, are on their trail, and suddenly cats begin to vanish. Can Hayden and his troop put a stop to these mysterious disappearances before they mysteriously vanish, too?

For ages 12-18

The Ghosts of Northwood Cemetery**—**When Greg Logan takes his girlfriend Karen on a late night walk-through of Northwood Cemetery, Karen is spooked by the silence, the darkness, and something she sees but can't explain. When they meet with two other teenagers in the cemetery, strange things begin to happen. Greg and Karen can't rest until they figure out the meaning of the strange goings-on in the Northwood Cemetery.

For ages 13-up

The Mountaintop**—**Jason, a seventeen-year-old Amerian, sets out for the mountaintop to determine the truth of his people's beliefs. On his journey he runs into some unexpected and eye-opening adventures. Most importantly, he meets Manda, a 17-year-old Ginder girl, who changes his life irrevocably.

For Adults

Hobson's Planet**—**When Culp Robinson arrives on the Hobson's Planet, he steps into a whirlwind of controversy and political upheaval. Against his will, Culp finds himself the designated savior to another planet. Having failed on Earth, he wants no part of another such quest. Now he must decide where his duty and his heart lie.

Ant-Nee's Golden Notebook**—** Mayhem and mix-ups follow Bruno Brunotaglia's murder of a hit man sent after him by a rival mob. Panic stricken, Bruno leaves behind a briefcase of money and an import notebook. Two down-and-out friends find the briefcase and notebook, and Bruno needs them back before his father, head of the Philly mob, blows a gasket. Will Richard get to keep the briefcase of money he found with Strangler and the Indian hard on his trail? Can Clarence make hay from the information in the notebook? It's a battle of half-wits in this deadly game of hide and seek.

Henny and Lloyd: Private Eyes—Henny and Lloyd, age mid-twenties, have completed their online course in private detecting and are now licensed PIs. They've rented an office on Centre Street in downtown NYC, a rundown apartment each in Williamsburg, Brooklyn, and now set out to make their dreams of crime-fighting come true.

The Sad Case of Brownie Terwilliger—Brownie Terwilliger looks at his opportunity of running for mayor of Philadelphia as a chance to right the wrongs of a city. He hopes to oust Milton Streezo, the incumbent, but Streezo does not take kindly to this challenge and concocts a plan to destroy Brownie, even hiring Lunky Ledbetter, famed perpetrator of dirty political tricks. Can Brownie withstand the onslaught? Will he have the opportunity to do some good in the world? Don't bet on it.

The Collected Short Stories - A man buried alive; the extinction of a gloried species; the mingling of interstellar races; a mysterious amulet; a fearful child; an animal-loving old hag; the assassination of the Almighty. Stories of horror, mystery, fantasy, and science fiction certain to raise the hairs on your neck.

The Rest is Silence—The Shakespeare Murders Vol 1 - When a body is found on the stage of the Bouwerie Lane Theatre, the AWB Theatre is thrown into turmoil, and Don Lovett, one of its actors, is suspected of murder. Can AWB actor Mark Louis exonerate his good friend and bring the life of the acting troupe back to normal?

A Dying Fall - The Shakespeare Murders Vol 2 - When the AWB Theatre Company accepts an invitation to perform on the tropical island of Illyria, they get more than they bargained for. Sudden death. Mark Louis, company member and amateur detective, suspects murder. The actors, however, must return home to New York, forcing Mark to conduct his investigation a thousand miles from the crime.

To Prove a Villain - The Shakespeare Murders Vol 3 -When Mark Louis investigates the death of Kristy King's brother, what he learns upends their theatre company as well as his relationship with Kristy. Should he have let sleeping dogs lie?

A Spider Steeped—The Shakespeare Murders Vol 4 - Mark Louis and Kristy King become involved with murder when they visit Erin Blakely, a college friend of Kristy's whom she hasn't seen in half-a-dozen years. Hoping to uncover the truth about Erin's tangled life, Mark and Kristy decide to investigate four men from Erin's past and present.

A Summer Murder—Three months at the beach with friends and with a young lady named Eileen Meredith, the blonde beauty of the summer. A young woman to die for? No, a young woman to be murdered. For adults.

Henny and Lloyd's Best Cases - Henny and Lloyd, Private Eyes, solve some of the most baffling cases of their newly-launched careers.

Henny and Lloyd's Casebook - Henny and Lloyd are hard at work tracking down wrongdoers of all sorts in cases that would baffle the ordinary detective, and our two heroes are anything but ordinary.

Writing as Paul Johns:

From Out the Shadowed Night—How far would you go to achieve revenge? Brian Martin committed an unspeakable crime and managed to escape responsibility for his act. Now, sixteen years later, not only do the effects of his crime rise up out of the past, but something much more deadly begins to haunt him as well.

Prayer Preyer —Fifty years of obstacles have kept Jerry Curtis from locating Father Lockhart. Now, he's found the priest and is determined to take his revenge for the crime committed against him all those years ago.

Dear reader,

I hope you've enjoyed reading this adventure of Henny and Lloyd, private eyes.

Your opinion is valuable to other
readers like you,
who may be looking for books like mine.

Please consider taking a few minutes to post a review,
however brief,
on the site where you purchased this book
or on the Wings ePress web page.

You may also want to visit my author page
at the Wings' website where you can find the complete
collection of my books, including the others in the Henny
and Lloyd series.

Thank you!

John Paulits

Visit Our Website
For The Full Inventory
Of Quality Books:

Wings ePress, Inc

Quality trade paperbacks and downloads
in multiple formats,
in genres ranging from light romantic comedy to general
fiction and horror.
Wings has something for every reader's taste.
Visit the website, then bookmark it.
We add new titles each month!

Wings ePress, Inc.
3000 N. Rock Road
Newton, KS 67114

Made in the USA
Columbia, SC
02 September 2024